THE RED STORM

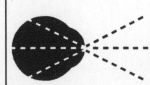

This Large Print Book carries the
Seal of Approval of N.A.V.H.

THE RED STORM

GRANT BYWATERS

THORNDIKE PRESS
A part of Gale, Cengage Learning

GALE
CENGAGE Learning·

Farmington Hills, Mich • San Francisco • New York • Waterville, Maine
Meriden, Conn • Mason, Ohio • Chicago

GALE
CENGAGE Learning

Thorndike Press® Large Print Crime Scene.
The text of this Large Print edition is unabridged.
Other aspects of the book may vary from the original edition.
Set in 16 pt. Plantin.

LIBRARY OF CONGRESS CATALOGING-IN-PUBLICATION DATA

Names: Bywaters, Grant, author.
Title: The red storm / by Grant Bywaters.
Description: Large print edition. | Waterville, Maine : Thorndike Press, 2016. | ©
   2015 | Series: Thorndike Press large print crime scene
Identifiers: LCCN 2015047357| ISBN 9781410488183 (hardcover) | ISBN 1410488187
   (hardcover)
Subjects: LCSH: Private investigators—Fiction. | New Orleans (La.)—History—20th
   century—Fiction. | Louisiana—Race relations—Fiction. | Large type books. |
   GSAFD: Mystery fiction.
Classification: LCC PS3602.Y93 R43 2016 | DDC 813/.6—dc23
LC record available at http://lccn.loc.gov/2015047357

Published in 2016 by arrangement with St. Martin's Press, LLC

Printed in Mexico
1 2 3 4 5 6 7 19 18 17 16

To the memory of Kurt Bywaters.
Not a day goes by I don't think of you.
Miss you, Dad.

ACKNOWLEDGMENTS

I would like to thank my wife, Heidy, and my family, as well as my editor, Jennifer Letwack, for all her help in making this book happen.

CHAPTER 1

The first time I met Bill Storm was in New York in the early part of what would become known as the Roaring Twenties. I was broke then, making little money boxing. That night I was in a heavyweight bout against some pugilist Italian named Horace Francisco. The purse had been set at thirty dollars: twenty-five to the winner and five to the loser.

Not satisfied with the money being offered, I told the promoter that I would not even bother suiting up unless he promised to give me a cut of the gate receipts. He refused, and delicately explained to me that if I did not get my "black ass" in the ring, I would not leave the venue alive. I believed him.

Nonetheless, it was a sure shot I'd be making off with most of the purse. I was so confident of the win, if not bored at the competition I was getting, that I did little training or roadwork to prepare for it. With a record of 52 wins, 2 draws, and 50 knockouts — my only three defeats coming from debatable decisions — it was hard to find suitable opponents. It did not matter that most legit rankings had me ranked in the top three of heavyweights; I had the misfortune of having heavy hands. This made promoters and managers of name contenders avoid me because the last thing they wanted to see was their cash cows sprawled out on the canvas.

The only thing Horace had going for him tonight was having a longer reach than me. At six foot one his reach was measured at the weigh-ins from fingertip to fingertip as seventy-eight inches, while at the same height mine was seventy-six.

He was able to survive the first few rounds because he boxed me, staying on the outside and using his extra reach to his benefit. In the end, his ego got the best of him. After being on the receiving end of a few nasty jabs to the face, he moved the fight inside, where I went at him with pinpoint combinations.

I dropped him twice midway through the rounds. First was with a vicious left hook that knocked him through the ropes and into a spectator's lap. The second time was with a right-left-right combination. The referee pulled me over to a neutral corner and stalled the count the best he could. He did everything outside of putting Horace's gloves on and fighting me himself to get him back in the fight. The delay was enough for Horace's head to clear by the count of eight, and he got up on wobbling legs.

He clenched, ran, and danced until the final round in an attempt to decision me. The seconds worked me over in my corner before the final bell, while my manager, Karl Monroe, in his habitual Panama hat, leaned into my ear and said "You managed to bust up his left eye in that last round, and it's starting to swell over. He's probably got a blind spot there. So keep hitting it. You're the puncher, so you need to go in there and outgun him. Cut that ring off like I told you so he can't keep punching and runnin' like he's been doing. Don't leave it up to them judges to make the decision, because you know they'll go against you."

He was right. Even though the Walker Law had ended the no-decision days when, in a futile attempt to rid the sport of corrupt judging, a fight was won only by a knockout, I still needed to win by one. If left to the judges, it'd end in a "majority draw" at best. It made little difference to them that I landed more clean, effective punches, or that I scored two knockdowns and had not a scratch on me. The same could not be said about Horace. His face looked like it'd been shoved into an airplane propeller.

At the start of the bell, Monroe shoved in the gum shield and I leapt toward Horace, who again played it safe. He jabbed and retracted, jabbed and retracted. I swung at him, but he used his lateral movement to evade me. His constant running away annoyed me enough that I hit him with a haymaker that sent him against the ropes. When I closed in, he head-butted me and then hit me below the belt. In pain, I looked over at the referee, who along with the crowd ignored the fouls, and so did the crowd.

Irate, I threw out all notions of going easy on him and charged after him until I bullied him into a corner. There was no longer anyplace for him to run and hide. I sent hooks and jabs into his eye until there wasn't an eye left, and then focused on his jaw. The referee stepped in, pulled me off, and called the fight. The crowd was on its feet and shook the arena with a prolonged roar of disapproval.

In my respected corner, Monroe went between the ropes and leaned in to me.

"Sweet Jesus, what the hell was that?"

I shrugged.

"I'll be surprised if he'll ever be able to see clear out of that eye again. Probably shattered his eye socket, and his jaw don't look too good, either."

Horace was crammed in his corner with the ringside doctor bandaging him up. I went over to mitt him, but Horace didn't get up off his stool.

From a swollen mouth he said, "You fight dirty, Fletcher. I had this fight and you know it."

"You best get that eye and jaw looked at."

Horace leaned over his stool and spit a mouthful of blood at my feet. "Better give me a rematch. If you don't, you're a coward because you know I'll lay you flat in the first."

I didn't argue with him that it was a one-sided fight, and he was lucky not to have gotten more hurt than he already was. The audience was still frantic.

I went to my corner, where Monroe was waiting. "You done fine, kid. He had this fight dead fixed for him to win. Had his own referee, and I heard his manager paid two of them judges off."

"I'm tired of fighting these palookas that got no business being in the ring with me,"

I said. "At least I still got my shot against the champ."

"Nothing doing on that one, kid," Monroe said. "I didn't want to tell you before the fight, but I spoke with the champ's manager a few hours ago. He's pretty sure now that he don't stand a chance against you. But the champ said he don't want to hand over his strap to a nigger and that's all there is to it."

This was not the first time I had been denied my shot against the belt. No promoter was going to let a colored like Jack Johnson, the first black heavyweight champion, to ever again run off with the most coveted crown in sports. Not when Jack London's call for a "Great White Hope" to defeat Johnson had proved to be so difficult.

"What'd I got to do? Murder one of these pugs in the ring to get my shot with the champ?"

With disgust, I ripped the last glove off my hand myself and went to change. When I had finished yanking into my togs, I left the boxing pavilion. A tall man who looked like the missing link between man and primate approached me.

"I've been watching you for a while, kid. You got a pair of hands, and I've been thinking of using a guy like you."

No introduction was needed. I knew who he was. Most folks in the area did. Bill Storm was a prominent heavy who local syndicates hired out to do muscle work. Even back then he was aging. What hair he had left was starting to gray. Lines were outlining obliquely along his grill, which almost certainly was never handsome to begin with. His nose had been broken so many times it went off in several different directions. No matter, his cold gray eyes showed there was life left in him. They burned with a brutal hatred and a primal urge for violence.

"I don't think I'd be interested in your kind of work," I said. "I'm sure you can find some poor colored that doesn't mind getting thrown into the grinder when the time comes for a fall guy."

Storm laughed. "Look here, kid. I don't sell out anyone that works for me. One thing that means more to me than anything, even more than money and dames, is loyalty. Do straight with me, and I'll as soon as take the fall myself than sell you out."

I expected him to say something like that. Most of his kind did. However, I knew there was rarely loyalty among his type of crowd.

"What'd you need me for anyway? Seems you been doing just fine by yourself," I said.

15

"Sure I was, when I was younger. Now mugs are getting the idea that age has slowed me down, and trying to take a pop at me when they never would've had the backbone before. It's a mistake on their part, I assure you, but my job is mostly intimidation, see. My employers don't like seeing their customers constantly gettin' roughed up. But if I had a bird like you with me, they'd think twice about getting cute."

Massaging my sore knuckles, I did not know whether to believe a word he was saying. Being a clever man, he quickly picked up on this.

"Look here, kid. I'm offering you a chance to make some real dough. I figured you'd be tired of busting yourself up over chicken feed. You're the one doing all the fighting, but them promoters and everyone else is making the money, not you. So you got to decide whether you want to keep making other people rich for the rest of your life or rise above it."

That's how it went. A partnership had been formed, more or less. For the next few months I worked alongside Storm, mostly as backup, or as a stand-in. We made our rounds, collecting payments for various syndicates. Most of the time, the people paid up, from gambling receipts to "protection" payments. Sometimes, they'd get wise, but often would back down when they realized Storm and I were gearing up to do major violence to them.

I made more money than I ever did before. It was more than I was getting paid doing boxing exhibitions, which were nothing but glorified sparring sessions between fights to supplement what little I was getting boxing. Instead of spending it on women and booze, which Storm advised I do, I put it away. I spent very little. I moved out of the flophouse I was living in and moved to a place in Harlem that was somewhat better. With just 750 square feet and plumbing and heating that sometimes worked, it was as good of housing a colored could get at the time. Segregation had a funny way of limiting one's options.

I did not tell Storm I was putting the cash away. I got the impression that if I did, he'd start getting worried I'd ditch him as soon as I got enough dividends stocked up. Presumably, that was why he always encouraged me to spend it as soon as I got it. Things were going sound, but I knew it would not last. Business never stayed efficient with guys like Storm. If it got too calm, he'd make sure to create some sort of disturbance. His temperament dictated that he needed chaos to thrive.

At the outset it started off with him roughing up people when he didn't need to. That escalated to him throwing a local store owner out a window and onto a couple of dames strolling by. This of course did not please the syndicates. There was no point in telling Storm he was burning his bridges. He was beyond reason at that point.

He progressively became more violent. When a restaurant manager refused to pay for any more protection, Storm wrenched him into the back room and grilled the right side of the man's mug on a scalding oven top.

In a short time our rounds dwindled. Storm had developed into too much of a liability for the syndicates and they were cutting his services off. Instead of picking up the hint, he kept at it until there were no more rounds to make.

I went weeks without even hearing from him, until he called me at my flat late one night. I had been waiting for such a call. I knew it had been weeks since our final rounds were made, and that Storm had been blacklisted by everyone that mattered. He likely hadn't been paid as of that time, which meant he was getting desperate.

18

"Hey kid, you busy?"

"Depends," I said. "What're you up to?"

"What makes you think I'm up to something?"

I didn't say anything.

"I need your help, just for tonight."

"Help doing what?"

"I'm finished here. It's time to get out. But I'm flat, see. I need some traveling dough so I can blow this burg. I got it all set up, see. It's nothing big, I just need you to watch someone for me while I see about collecting the heavy sugar. Don't worry, I plan on cutting you in on it if you help me out."

Being "cut in" was not what I was worried about. The "I need you to watch someone" was. I hung up the phone after getting directions to where he was at, and set out.

He gave me the location of a dive in Brooklyn. The commute took me more than an hour, and I arrived to the putrid stink of raw sewage from the Gowanus Canal. Shore birds flew from the weed-covered bank with large chunks of rotten meat, while horns of barges that crossed the commercial waterway sounded.

When Storm opened the door to his room on the top floor, I could tell he hadn't slept in days. Dark circles had fashioned around

19

his eyes, but they still lit with hatred and menace.

"What's this all about?" I demanded upon him leading me into the place.

He didn't say anything right away. He casually drew out the silver hip flask he always had filled with assortments of illicit alcohol, took a pull, and held it out for me. I refused his offer.

He finally said, "I need you to watch the kid while I go collect the dough."

"What kid?" I asked, but I had already ascertained the answer.

It was all over the papers. Some rich high-society couple's ten-year-old son had been kidnapped the previous day outside the hotel they were staying at. The couple was very prominent and had enough pull to get almost every copper in the city diverting their attention to finding junior.

"I got desperate," he said. "I needed dough. Someone told me about this kid, and how his folks are loaded. So I scoped out the joint they were at, and it was a cinch. The stupid kid was outside with his handler. He was cake to take out. They were walking to the store and I just got up behind him, and I guess I got a little too rough with the sissy. I accidentally broke his neck. The kid started yapping, but he was easy to shut up!"

"Where's the kid now?"

Storm nudged his head toward the back room. "He's asleep. I called his folks last night from a drugstore pay phone. Told them I wanted three G's, and where to drop it off tonight."

"You fool, you'll never get a piece of that kale! They'll have that place swarming with buttons. They're not going to risk that you ain't going to kill the kid after you have been paid off. They'll take their chance of beating the whereabouts out of you!"

"Got to risk it. I ain't kickin', I'm in desperate shape. Besides, I can smell them bulls a mile off. If I'm left holding the bag, I'll make damn sure to send them parents a piece of junior to show them I wasn't foolin'!"

If it was anyone else, their threats would have come off as nothing more than hot air. But coming from Storm, I believed him, and there was no point in trying to reason with him. I had to make sure that his threat didn't become a reality, so I agreed to watch the kid while he left to collect.

When Storm had gone, I went inside the room to check up on the kid, and to make sure he wasn't dead. Luckily, he wasn't. He

21

had tucked himself away in the far corner of the room. When I hit the lamps, he covered his eyes with his arms like a bat using its wings to shield itself from the emanating light.

"It's okay, kid. I ain't going to hurt you. What's your name?"

He was nonresponsive. I stood there for a bit watching him, until at length he took his arms away from his eyes. He was a cute kid, with full blond hair, chubby trumpeter's cheeks, and a boyish face.

I left the room, but kept the door ajar. I sat on the couch, glancing at my railroad-grade pocket watch. As more time went by, the chance that things had gone south intensified. There could only be one possibility, Storm had gotten pinched and was being put through the wringer by the law. The city kitties would try to rough him up, but would end up hurting themselves more than Storm. The only shot they had to get Storm to sing was if it did Storm some good to do so. Like a lesser charge. That would mean the place would be raided by flatfoots at any moment. Either way, both outcomes were bad.

I got to my feet and went back into the room. "All right, time to beat it, kid," I said.

The kid was still impassive. It was more

than simple shock. I could not put my finger on it, but there was something odd with the kid. I had to shake him a few times to snap him out of it.

"Did you hear what I said?"

He didn't say anything. Impatient, I picked him up and flung him out the door as if he was a stray cat. When he had gotten to his feet, they moved without thought, and carried him straight out of the flat. I listened as his footsteps picked up speed down the hall until the noise tapered off.

It was less than half an hour later that Storm came crashing into the flat, his red-veined eyes pumping with animalistic furry.

"You were right. The place was swarming with buzzards. They must figure I'm some sort of sap. I got to get out tonight, but not before I send the kid home worse than when I got him."

I didn't stand in the way as he went barging into the back room. It took but a few seconds for him to come back with even more hatred than before.

"Where the hell is the kid?"

"I let him go."

"You what!"

"I let him go," I said.

His attack was rapid enough that I had little time to counter a wild fist that was

23

heaved at me. Even though Storm was much bigger, my advantage was that I happened to have more power and faster hand speed. Storm swung at me with everything he had, and I did my best to duck or avoid the full contact of the blows.

Between slips, I tried to get hits in, but I might as well have hit a concrete wall with a rubber mallet. I switched it up, and victimized his kidneys and body, using my back foot as leverage to put more power behind my lead hand.

The fight kept on at an unyielding pace. The furniture, walls, fixtures, and anything else that had the misfortune of being present in the room were destroyed. Ultimately the pain caught up to Storm. His stamina was slowing while his blows were getting weaker and loopy.

That's when Storm hit that last burst of desperate rage that large beasts have when they know their end is near. I didn't see it coming, so I went for the power punches to finish him off. It was a risky move and often left you vulnerable to counters. Storm knew this, for he had once dabbled in prizefighting. When Storm had nothing left to hold him up but his shoelaces, I went in for the kill and threw a hard left. Storm hit me with a counterpunch with his potent right that sent me just about through the back wall.

I didn't black out, but time seemed to slow. Trying to regain my separated senses, I could see Storm sitting on the other side of the room. He was wheezing, and blood was coming out his mouth.

"I thought you were better than that, kid," he said.

"Don't be blaming me, you louse! You dug yourself into this. If you thought I'd sit by and let you kill some kid, that's just you being a fool."

Storm laughed, which seemed to pain him. We sat like that for a while, until the distant sound of sirens came into earshot.

"That brat must've called us in," he said, as he stumbled back onto his feet. Maybe the kid did give us up, but it was more likely Storm was followed. No matter, I didn't even attempt to get up. I merely watched as Storm lumbered toward the door. But before he left, he turned to me and said, "I'll be seeing you."

I do not know how I was able to get back up and duck out before the law took the building down. I do remember lying low in my flat for weeks. I had more than enough money to sit on. I read the papers, and found that the boy was safely returned to his parents. As for Storm, the papers reported that he had stolen a switch engine and killed the driver and two flatfoots during his escape out of town. The police had put a dragnet out for him, but it was too late. Storm had slipped through and vanished.

That was the last time I heard or saw Bill Storm, until he walked into a New Orleans diner more than fifteen years later.

CHAPTER 2

It was 1938, the sort of clear, sunny day that made living in New Orleans pleasant. I was sitting alone at a diner I often frequented, staring out the window, watching nothing in particular, and chewing over my choice of work. There hadn't been any clients in some time. But that was to be anticipated. I was limited to taking on mainly other coloreds as clientele, since accepting white clients almost always led to problems down the line.

The waitress, a rotund woman, topped my cup off while I aimlessly worked on the daily crossword puzzle in front of me. I was in the middle of trying to find a name of a web-footed bird that was five letters when a gravelly voice asked, "Mind if I sit with you?" With indifference, I didn't look up from the crossword, but instead said, "Whatever you got to do, friend. I was about to go anyway."

27

It was when the man had seated himself and his looming shadow fell across me that I looked up. I had to almost lean all the way back in the booth to get him in full view. He was still tall, and big, yet his face was unrecognizable. Only the gray, hate-filled eyes I recognized. Even after all these years, they were impossible to forget.

His face was sunken in and his skin was an embalmed gray color. His hair had fallen out long ago, leaving him bald and looking like a lopsided baseball.

"Hello, Champ. Been a long time," he said in a voice that sounded like a crowbar going through a meat grinder.

"Yes, it sure has," I said.

"It hurts just walking these days."

I didn't know whether he wanted sympathy out of me or not. If he did, he wasn't going to get it.

"What can I do for you, Storm?"

He laughed, but like the last time I saw him laugh, it seemed to cause him discomfort.

"Why couldn't you ever just call me Bill?"

"If we were pals, I might've. But we never were pals."

"No, I suppose we weren't. I figure I was a bit crazy back then."

"I ain't in any sort of mood to swap stories

28

from way back when. Either you tell me your business, or I'm going to pay my bill and blow on out of here."

"Hey, don't be like that. I came here because I need your services, you playin' detective and all. If you don't want to do it, just consider it evening the score."

"There's no score to even. If you still think I played you, that's your problem, not mine."

"Okay, fine. But at least hear me out. I can't even take a leak anymore without pissing blood after what you did to me that night. Surely that's worthy of you hearing me out, ain't it?"

"You got about the time it'll take me to finish my coffee and pay the bill," I said.

"It's like I was saying, I need your services. I heard you were playing detective these days, and I still can't wrap my head around that one. I tried lookin' you up, but you ain't listed and you don't got no office."

"I reckon this is as good of an office as any."

"And cheap rent, just a cup of joe, am I right?" he asked.

I said, "Why don't you just get on with what you want from me."

"I need you to help me find my daughter."

It took a lot to surprise me. Yet here I was,

surprised. I suppose the thought of him having a daughter made him almost human.

"I had her years before we ever met. Hooked up with some crazy dame, found out she was pregnant. Funny part is, I wanted nothing to do with having no kid, that is until the first time I saw her. Hard as it may seem, I was gonna go legit for that kid. Try to be some sort of decent father. But that didn't happen, see. I came home to my flat to find out the witch took the kid and scrammed. Left this note saying she didn't want a monster like me having anything to do with her child. It's funny how she didn't think of me that way when I had them legs wrapped around my neck. Doing the kinda stuff that got her knocked up in the first place. But I guess that's dames for you."

"How old would she be now?"

Storm inclined forward in his seat. "I figure she's gotta to be in her late twenties by now."

"Let's get to the part of you coming to me."

"I had been looking for her for years now. I almost lost hope of ever finding her, until a friend of mine who knew the witch told me he saw her here less than a year ago. Said he thinks she lives here. If she's here,

30

it's a sure bet so is my daughter. When I found out you were working as a dick in this area as well, I figure things were working out just right."

"Just right for what?"

"Look at me, kid; I ain't gonna last much longer. I'm all busted up on the inside. Last doctor I saw said that I'd be lucky to live another year or two. I just got to see my kid before I check out."

It was hard to see Storm being emotional. The most emotion I ever saw out of him was a sadistic pleasure that came with inflicting pain onto people. Age had either made him soft, or that daughter of his had always been his weak spot.

"Let's say I want to help, which I honestly don't, I can't. I can only hire on colored clients, see. If I started hiring white clients, it'd only cause more trouble than I already have. Besides, you're a felon. Don't think I didn't read about them John Laws you killed busting out of town."

Storm didn't say anything for a while. In time he scooted out of the booth and got on his feet. "I reckon you're right, kid. Don't want to cause you no troubles. I just figure you could do a little lookin' around for me, under the table. If you turn up something or if you don't, I'd still pay you good for your time. I got plenty of dough to throw around."

"Is it hot?"

"Not anymore it ain't," he said, pulling out a wad of bills.

"Keep your damn confetti. I'm not interested in your blood money."

"All money is blood money, kid."

"I don't want nothin' linkin' you to me. I'll do some looking around for you this afternoon, see what I can find, but that's it. After today, I don't ever want to see your mug again."

"Fair enough," he said.

"Does the mother have a name, besides 'the witch'?"

"Frieda Rae."

"Where did this person you know see Miss Rae at?"

"He said he saw her leaving some store at North Robertson and Canal. I checked it out myself, but I couldn't get nothing."

"And you say he saw her less than a year ago?"

"That's right."

"Does this person that saw her have a name?"

"No, he don't."

"This doesn't have to do with that whole loyalty jive of yours, does it?"

"Maybe."

I didn't press the matter. It was worthless, too. "You wouldn't have a photograph of Mrs. Rae, by any chance?"

"I figured you'd ask me that. Yeah, I do."

He jerked a worn leather wallet out his front coat pocket. From inside he took out a three-by-five photograph and handed it to me. It was an old black-and-white photo of a nude woman with her back toward the camera. She was sitting on her feet, with her head turned back toward the lens in a tantalizing manner. Her black hair cascaded down the curves of a shapely back. Above her left shoulder blade was a minute tattoo of a lightning bolt.

"Quite a knockout, wasn't she?" Storm asked. "She told me she wanted to be a model, so I took a few photographs of her. This is the only one I have. She took them all when she did the run-out, except this one. I always kept it in my wallet."

The photograph probably wouldn't be much help. It was doubtful that Miss Rae would even look remotely close to the way she did from a photograph that was taken nearly a lifetime ago. Outside of that, the photo would be viewed by most people as obscene or inappropriate at the least. This would make it hard to even show the photo to anyone that might recognize her.

"Where are you staying at so I can contact you later?"

"I'll give you a number," he said. I handed him the pencil I was using for the crossword. He wrote his number on a blank margin in the paper. "I'll be waitin' for that call."

I didn't say anything as he left the diner. Instead, I sat at the table for a bit, wondering if I should just finish the crossword, go home, and call him later saying it was a dead end. I didn't feel any moral obligation to help him out, chiefly because I took no material compensation from him, outside of getting him out of my hair. But the desire to get out and do some sort of work after such a long delay was overwhelming.

I glanced out the window once more, expecting to see the same clear sky I had been gawping at a just a bit earlier. Instead, all I saw was gray.

CHAPTER 3

There was only one person that could have given Storm the dope on his old lady, and that was Rollie Lavine. Lavine was Storm's lackey in New York. Back then he was a freckle-faced kid that did whatever Storm told him to do or, as Storm put it, "He's my monkey and I'm his grinder." When Storm fled, Lavine leeched onto me and followed me to New Orleans.

I'd stayed away from him for most of the intervening years, even though he did his best to not make it so. The last I heard from him, he was fencing goods among other things.

I parked my 1937 Ford Club Coupe on Napoleon Avenue, in front of the one-bedroom cottage where Lavine was living.

The cottage was rotting with siding stripped off from the humidity like peeled rinds. I knocked on the door several times. I knew Lavine was there. He was nocturnal, and spent his days sleeping.

It took much pounding on the door before a "Who the hell is it?"

"It's Fletcher."

"I'm sleepin'. Get lost."

"Open the damn door or I'll break it down."

The door opened and Lavine stood just inside the entryway. His eyes were tired and bloodshot. His auburn hair had once been a full mop, but it had thinned and lost most of its volume. He was wearing gray khakis and a stained yellowish undershirt.

"What'd you want?" he said.

I didn't answer, but forced my way in. Clutter littered the flyblown main room and I had to kick things aside to clear a path. Along the wall sat a secondhand single-cushion sofa. Its upholstery was worn so thin that springs and stuffing protruded out. In front of the sofa a wooden crate stood in for a coffee table. A collection of drug and smoking paraphernalia, including a bag of rolling tobacco with an Indian chief on the front, a pipe, lamp, dispensers made of porcelain and a ladle, items all used for opium, were scattered on top of it. Insufficient ventilated air suffocated the room. It smelled of sweat, stale tobacco, and human decay. The unfurnished kitchen had a single-burner stove that had not been in use in some time. Old newspapers and mail were stacked on top in a state of disarray.

"If I'd known you were comin'," he said, "I'd have picked the joint up."

"Sure you would've," I said. "I want to talk to you, but not in here. This place is downright disgusting."

He led me through the back door, which went into a courtyard that was stone-walled in to shield it from its adjoining neighbors. I took a seat at a wrought-iron patio table. Lavine accompanied me, but could not disguise his annoyance.

"What's dis all about?"

"I want to ask you a few questions," I said.

"Suppose I don't feel like answerin' them?"

"Suppose you start thinkin' about your health because you're startin' to piss me off!"

He tried his best to not sound intimidated. "Aw, you can't scare me. You ain't a fighter no more! You gettin' old and soft."

"Do I look soft?"

"No," he said. "But you ain't lookin' too good either. I didn't think you could get any uglier. All them hits to the face done a number on it."

"We ain't here to talk about my beauty," I

37

said. "You been keeping in contact with our old friend."

"Who's that?"

"You know damn well who it is," I said.

"You talkin' about Bill Storm? I haven't chatted it up with him since he went on the lam."

"Stop talkin' out of your hat, Rollie," I said. "Storm came to see me this morning. Said someone here tipped him off about seeing his old lady. You're the only one in these parts that would know who he is, besides me."

"Okay, so I jawed it up with him once in a while, they ain't no crime in that."

"Except he's a known fugitive that bumped off two cops," I said. "How'd you stay in contact with him?"

"By wire. I couldn't mail him nothin' because he'd move around so much, and he never left no forwarding addresses. He'd just send me a wire from time to time, askin' about things. I told him how I thought everyone here was crazy, but you got to be crazy living in a city that's six feet below the river."

"Nobody asked you to come here," I said.

"Yeah, I know that. Storm said the same thing. He also asked about you."

"What'd you tell him?"

"Nothin' much, seein' as you don't ever talk to me. I told him you turned shamus. He didn't believe me at first."

"Of course he didn't," I said. "You told him you saw his girl on Canal. Is that legit or was it a ploy to get him to come out here?"

"It's on the cuff. I met her before she took off. Real fine piece of leg, but I told Storm she can't be trusted, and he best keep her on a leash or somethin'. I wasn't surprised when she ditched him. That's just women for you. They ain't worth trustin' at all."

"You sound like you're talking from experience," I said.

"I am. See, I learned real fast about dames. Did you know I was married once?"

I shook my head. I was married once too in what now seemed like another life. I tried to picture what she looked like, but couldn't. Too many hits to the head, perhaps.

"Yeah, it was a long time ago," he continued. "I was just nineteen, and she was a real catch, if you get what I'm sayin'. But when we got hitched things were different. Nothin' was good enough for her, see, and she spent the dough faster than I could earn it. Started racking up debts, until I cut her off. Thought that'd be the end of it, but I come home to find she stole my stash and shoved off. Didn't see her again until a few years later when she came around asking for money. Said she owed some fat cats a lot."

"Did you help her out?" I asked.

"Hell no. Told her she could go whore herself out for the cash. She cried and blubbered, but I didn't give her a dime, see. Not one goddamn dime. I figured that'd be the last I'd be hearin' from her till I get word from her sister that she went off and hanged herself. I still got her obituary tacked up somewhere inside. It gives me a good laugh every time I come across it."

"You are a bitter, ugly, little man, Rollie," I said.

He shrugged. "I've been called worse."

With not much to go on, I had to take to the streets for leads. I hugged the curb adjacent to the small market stand on North Robertson and Canal, and gaited up to the elderly Creole man that was running the corner fruit stand. I showed him the photograph and it caused him to gape up at me in horror. He screamed an earful of vulgarity and told me to leave him alone, and that my business was not welcome.

I liked most French Creoles. They were far more accepting of coloreds, like France was. Plus, a lot of them shared African blood. Yet some had an overly pretentious attitude that grew maddening at such times as this.

I flashed the photo here and there to the local transients that panhandled the same spot for months. What I got for my troubles was responses like "Damn, if I ever saw that dish, I'd remember."

In the middle of flashing the photo to a blotto that was so bent that he could hardly stand on his own two feet, let alone focus on a picture, I heard: "Why, I know that woman."

I crooked around to see a short, older woman, with white-gold lorgnette folding glasses and a black woven straw hat with a wide dark taffeta ribbon.

"You do?" I asked.

"Why, yes. I only recognized her because I saw photographs of her similar to that one when I was helping box up her belongings."

"You were a friend of hers?"

"I wouldn't say we were close. We knew each other from going to the same church and functions. I volunteered to take care of her belongings after she passed away."

"How long ago did she pass?"

"It was only a few months ago, the poor dear."

41

"Did you know her daughter?" I asked.

"I saw her a few times, but I didn't know her well. Frieda tried to get her to go to church with her. She went a few times in the beginning, but never again. Too bad, it would have done her good. I heard she's singing at some shameful club on Bourbon Street. They play a lot of that jungle music there."

"Do you know which club?"

"Not offhand. I only recall this because a few of us from church were leaving flyers around there, to try and talk some sense into the unfortunate girls that work that street, when one of them saw her performing."

I thanked the woman and made my way to Bourbon.

The street was thirteen blocks I often avoided at night. By day, it was quiet and by all accounts just another street, but at night it was a different story. Soon as the neon lights came on, the street become a congested three-ring circus of criminals, whores, the promiscuous, drunks, and tourists.

The area was sort of the city's unofficial red-light district. The official one ran along Basin Street near the French Quarter and was known as Storyville. The sixteen blocks of vice got its nickname from a city councilman who wrote the ordinance. It was only when the famous Blue Book that listed more than seven hundred prostitutes got into the hands of the navy boys stationed nearby that the Secretary of the Navy was prompted to demand in 1917 that the area be closed. Yet it never really closed, it just moved elsewhere.

I stopped and tipped the kids that sidewalk tap-danced, and a few other local homeless men that worked the street. Most of them knew me. There was no room to be a lone wolf in my business. The types that went around demanding information out of people never lasted long. The truth of the matter is nobody is in a legal sense obligated to talk to a private detective or provide them with any information at all. Threatening, tricking, or making people think I was part of law enforcement to get information out of them was sure to land me in jail.

In order to make it, I needed to know and have contacts with as many people as possible. Those people ranged from powerful businessmen to barbers and all the way down to the regular homeless. In fact, I found the homeless to be the most helpful, since they knew the area the best, and were very observant about things.

Emanuel Morton was such a contact. Morton had lost his farm in Texas in foreclosure after his land blew away in the Dust Bowl. He came to New Orleans a broken refugee and a drunk. He got a job as a barker for a mixed bar on Bourbon. Unlike other barkers, whose methods bordered on harassment in an attempt to lure patrons into the establishments, Morton was friendly and struck up a conversation with everyone.

I made him sort of my operative with the instructions that he was no good to me drunk all the time. It was enough to get him to cut his drinking down.

I found him standing at his fixed spot on the corner of Conti Street. He was a big man, dwarfing even me. When he saw me coming, a wide, toothless grin came across his face.

"Ay, Will," he said, giving me a grip that would have crushed someone's hand if they weren't prepared for it.

"They seem to be keeping you busy all hours of the day," I said.

"Sure am. The boss says I can get some extra hours working early. Says people are startin' their drinkin' earlier every day."

"That ain't surprising, livin' in as rough times as we are."

44

"I'm mighty lucky I got me job and all when most folks don't. Mighty lucky."

"How's your drinking?"

"Fine. Went on the wagon few weeks ago. Haven't touched the stuff, honest to God."

"Good to hear." I handed him the photo. "I'm trying to get a locate on this woman's daughter. Heard she was workin' somewhere on this street."

Morton gave the photo a hard look and mumbled out as he tried to recollect, "Say . . . there is . . . uh . . . a . . . poster of a woman kinda looks like her just a few blocks up. 'Cept she got clothes on in her picture. Say, can I keep this?"

"No."

With great reluctance, he gave the photograph back.

"Be seein' you, Morton," I said. "Maybe when work picks up for me, I'll get you a few side jobs."

"Sure thing, boss," he said. "I could always use some extra money."

I found the place on Bourbon and St. Louis to be a "gentleman's club" called Le Familier Minou. On the substantial windows was an assortment of posters of the "dancers" and "singers." One of the placards was an attractive woman that looked unerringly like

45

the photograph of Frieda Rae. She had raven black hair, a stunning figure, and a talent for provocative poses. The name she went by was "Lady Storm!" The sign stated that she would be singing every night until the end of the week.

It was while I was looking this over that a tall, pug-faced doorman stepped out from inside the club.

"What time is Lady Storm performing tonight?" I asked.

"She'll be on stage a little past nine," he said. "But don't be getting the idea that you'll be seeing her. We don't allow your kind in here!"

In my younger, hotheaded days, those words would've been enough to start some trouble over. With age came enough smarts to know that it'd just get me nowhere but a night or more in the stir. At the very least, it would give the downtown boys the chance to run me out of town.

"I'll be here at nine," I said.

I left, but not before I heard, "I'll be waiting for you, sweetheart."

CHAPTER 4

With time to kill, I went back to my apartment on St. Ann and Royal Street in the French Quarter. D'Armes was a courtyard of bungalows and rooms. The French landlord of the establishment was generous enough to allow me to rent there, when most would not have. In return, I offered my services to him whenever he needed them, which he did now and then. The last time involved me tracking an ex-tenant who upon eviction destroyed his room, right down to the plumbing. I'd tracked him to a dive he cooped up at out in Baton Rouge. Through the use of blunt force more than diplomacy, I rolled him for the cost of the damages.

Things were shaky when I first moved in. Several longtime tenants packed up their belongings and left, and one went as far as threatening the landlord with murder if he didn't have me evicted. The landlord evicted him instead, and took advantage of the city's notoriously lax adherence to segregation laws and started renting the rooms out to well-off colored Creoles as well. It turned out to be more profitable for him, since many Creoles were willing to pay good money to live above what Jim Crow would allow.

There were a lot of wealthy coloreds in New Orleans. In slave times, the city was one of the few that had slaves doing skilled jobs, and was also home of the most free blacks in the country. After the Emancipation, many of the skilled coloreds prospered doing jobs ranging from carpenters to newspaper editors. It continued now because of the city's more lax view on segregation.

Inside my flat, I showered and ate an early dinner of leftover steak and potatoes that I had fixed up the previous evening.

I cleared the slop off my plate fast, and checked my watch. It was past six. I decided to call Brawley at his home. Brawley was a detective sergeant who had first worked in commercial crimes before being bumped up to the vice unit after success in lending his aid during the '29 streetcar strike that had resulted in a series of dynamite bombings, shootings, and assaults. In that division, he took part in the grandstanding campaign to rid the city of illegal gambling, prostitution, and drugs.

I had worked hard to get Brawley on my side. We weren't exactly friends, but we both knew we could help each other out. He granted me support, which was fundamental to the work I did. I never would have lasted this long without it. In return, I provided him with information from the colored community that most cops would be hard pressed to get. Doing pro bono jobs for fellow coloreds who didn't have a lot of money but had a lot of information had given me a lot of contacts through the years. Contacts in my work were as valuable as gold.

What sealed the deal with Brawley was me giving him information on a shipment of drugs coming into port, and what man was carrying them. This got him a big break, and headlines, busting a cripple coming off the boat that had stuffed pounds of heroin into his prosthetic leg.

But Brawley's true acceptance of me arose more from his heritage than anything. He was Jewish and the descendant of people that had fled the anti-Jewish violence in Eastern Europe to Ireland. Ireland was somewhat neutral in those days, but priests started holding sermons denouncing the Jewish community and depicting them as being a threat to their young. The success-ful boycott of Jewish tradesmen caused Brawley's family to uproot itself again, this time to New Orleans for work.

The phone rang several times before a husky woman's voice with a thick monotone Russian accent answered. Brawley's wife, Tamara.

"Da?"

"Is your husband there?"

"Vait moment, please," she said, and set the phone down. I could hear her over the line yelling for him. The phone fumbled around before a "Yeah" came over the line.

"It's Fletcher. What's going on?"

"Nothing outside of gettin' yelled out by my crazy wife."

He wasn't kidding; his wife was crazy, even more so when she drank and went into jealous rages that ended with her throwing things at him.

"You want to go out," I said.

"And go where?"

"I heard Le Familier Minou had some nice stuff to look at."

I heard him laugh over the line. "What time?"

"Nine."

"Fine, see you there at nine," he said, and hung up.

The same pug-faced doorman was standing outside the club when I got there. Brawley's bullish figure followed suit soon after. Brawley was a husk of muscle and extra weight. At five ten, he topped the scales out at around two-fifty. Because work had been slow, I had not seen Brawley in several months. He had lost a considerable amount of weight since I last saw him. No doubt, the missus had something to do with it.

We were about to step inside when the doorman blocked the entrance. "Like I told you earlier, we ain't taking your kind!"

Brawley grinned, realizing now why I had him come. He flashed his golden star and crescent-shaped badge to the doorman and said, "He's tagging along with me."

The doorman looked at the badge and said, "You can go, but your friend can't."

Brawley's friendly blue eyes switched to a cold mirthless scold as he cuffed the doorman's face with the back of his right hand. "That's some slow reflexes you got there, sonny," he said. "Reckon it wouldn't take much for my friend to knock you apart, and I got enough mind to let him do it if you don't get to stepping aside."

The doorman rubbed his reddish cheek, pouted, and shifted out of the way.

"Damn," Brawley said to me, "and here I was hoping he'd be stupid. Would've been more entertaining than what we're goin' to see in this dump."

A dive was the best word to describe what was inside. The place had everything you'd expect from such an establishment. It was furnished with a long, narrow bar complemented by tables that were aligned in front of a wooden stage, with the added touch of mood lighting. Men in all shapes and sizes and professions, from businessmen to street thugs, handed out money to the bevy of girls. The girls came in all varieties and all forms of undress. Some were in kinky lingerie, while others were as nude as the day they were born. Most of them were flour lovers, with so much face powder that it wore off on the men they were balling the jack with on the dance floor.

When we first stepped in, most of the men were distracted enough by the ladies and their carnal senses to notice my presence. We sat at a faraway unlit table to draw as little attention as possible. Before long, even the ones that had noticed me had all but forgotten about it with the presence of hot flesh pressed against them.

I sized up up the joint and found a few of the city's most prominent in the herd. One such person was Ruben Cristofani, who controlled a chunk of the illegal slot machine racket. I heard the bribe money he was throwing out to run the racket undisturbed was a fortune. Evidently he knocked over enough jack to shove it around, like in the cleavage of the vixen that was leaning over him.

Another jasper was Charlie Gains, a hophead who ran and sold every kind of drug that existed. His pal was Jerome Larson, a flesh peddler who had a side racket of blackmailing whites who slept with his stock of colored yes-girls.

The headwaiter kept avoiding our table, until Brawley got up and pulled him back by one of his ears.

"If this is what it takes to get some service around here, so be it."

Brawley let go of the man's ear. Shocked, the waiter said, "Sorry, mister, I didn't see you."

"The hell you didn't," Brawley said. "Just get us two coffees!"

Brawley, like me, rarely ever drank. Most smart cops didn't. "But ain't ya Irish?" was the response Brawley often got upon refusing a drink, which only made him more annoyed than he usually was.

When the headwaiter left, Brawley said, "Okay, I did my part and got you in here. Now it's your turn to put me in the picture. What's this all about?"

"I'm just here to see Storm sing."

Brawley grunted. "You think that's what she's goin' to be doin'? I been here enough times to know singing ain't all she'll be doin'."

No sooner had our drinks arrived than all the lights except the one on the stage went out. The piano player stepped on and started in on a generic jazzy number as Storm took the stage. She was wearing a stunning black beaded-lace evening dress that complemented her ebony hair. It was not hard to notice she looked faithfully like her mother, except for the cold, angry gray eyes she inherited from her old man.

She kicked off with some song that was breathy and seductive, but she was neither breathy nor seductive. Her singing was mediocre and her accompaniment lacked any sort of spontaneity. The piano player played the ivories as mechanized as an engine piston.

The crowd seemed to get as restless and bored as I was, and soon were yelling out, "Come on, take it off already!" Storm paid no attention to them. Her eyes were closed and she by all appearances was in a trance as she sung.

The yelling grew to be more frequent, until someone jumped onstage. He was a balding man that looked like he bathed himself daily in raw Crisco. He reached for the straps of Storm's dress while saying "Here, let daddy help you take it off."

The second he touched her, Storm snapped out of her spell, and looked at the man with the venomous eyes that were all too familiar to me. In a swift, catlike motion, she took a hold of the man's nether region with elongated claws, clamped onto it, twisted, and pulled straight out. The man screamed in atrocious agony and fell to the ground, weeping.

The crowd roared with a mix of laughter and rage. With haste, Storm ripped one of her spiked heels off and threw it into the mob, nearly impaling a man sitting close by.

Crisco was still blubbering on the stage when she stomped off backstage, all but ripping the stage curtain down in the process. The lights came on as the assembly vibrated with hubbub at what had occurred.

"Damn, I think I'm in love," Brawley said. He signaled the maître d' and flashed him his buzzer. "Tell the owner that I want to talk to him."

The maître d' left with a worried look. Within a few moments the manager, a short Frenchman with a sharp nose, small mouth, and a pencil mustache showed up.

"Officer. I can promise you that this is a respectable place. We do not tolerate what just transpired, and she will be terminated immediately, you have my promise on that."

"Easy there," Brawley said. "I like the kid. I want you to go fetch her for me, see? So I can kindly tell the lady that coming damn close to rippin' a man's balls off may not be the most civil or legal thing to do. And you might want to get that pervert onstage to a hospital."

"Yes, sir, I will see to it at once."

A moment after the Frenchman left, two men carried Crisco, still holding his groin and screaming, out. My thought was that they were not taking him to a doctor, but out the back door to be tossed.

Storm's daughter arrived at our table looking even more stunning up close. Her long hair was like the pelage of a panther that was in stark contrast to her pale complexion and lips as red as her father's sins. Her face was still flushed with rage, but her voice was calm.

"Okay, mister. I suppose you want to

56

throw me in the can over what I did. Can't say I blame you, but a girl gets tired of apes pawing her all the time, and I had my fill."

"You should think about changing crowds then, toots," Brawley said.

"I work better crowds, but I happen to be in a jam right now, and this place offered me a quick fix if I played canary. But I ain't goin' to strip."

"Yes, because you're above doing such a thing, right?"

"No, it would just take a lot more dough than what they offered me to do it."

Brawley laughed. "Take a seat, doll. I got to make a call. Chat it up with my friend, he don't bite."

Brawley stood up and left, but not before giving me a wink. At first we sat in silence. She did not seem to be too bothered sitting across from me. I could tell others in the room were none too pleased. Perhaps she liked making people unsettled, a contrarian of sorts.

I had not realized that I was boring into her until she said, "Okay, mind telling me why you are looking at me like that?"

"Sorry, it's just you're very pretty."

Flattery, even a poor attempt at it, was a good way of breaking the ice and getting someone comfortable enough to talk to you.

But she was a bit too jaded to be flattered.

"You're a riot. I know when men are checking me out. It's why I close my eyes through most of my songs. So I don't have to look out at a bunch of bums with nasty thoughts in their heads. But you, you're looking at me the same way someone looks at a car wreck."

I changed the subject. "Mind if I ask you what may seem as a random question?"

She rolled her eyes. "Sure, why not."

"What do you know about your father?"

If the question caught her off guard, she didn't show it. Instead she said, "Now that is a random question, and one I don't care to discuss with a complete stranger."

"You're right," I said. I pulled out my business card and slid it to her. "Now we're not complete strangers."

"How so? Because you gave me your card?"

"It's a start. That card tells more information than most folks get on a first meeting."

She laughed. "Shouldn't have put that much effort into it, mister . . ." She looked at the card again. "William Fletcher."

"And your name is?"

"Zella."

"Interesting name," I said, "but let's talk about your old man."

58

"I don't know hardly anything about him, except for what my ma told me. She said he was some kind of lowlife. That's about it."

"I'd agree with that, having known the man and all," I said.

For the first time that night, Zella started showing signs of interest. "You're full of it, mister. If this is some ruse to seduce me or something, you're way off."

"It isn't," I said.

"Either way, I don't believe you."

I shrugged. "Fair enough, but if I was selling you a bill of goods, where do you suppose I got this?"

I handed her the three-by-five photograph. She said nothing as she stared with a vacant look at the picture.

"My, my. Ma had quite the figure back then," she finally said. "Okay, say I do believe you. What's this all about?"

"Your old man came here looking for you. Been looking for you for some time, or so he claims. Asked me if I could help locate you."

"I guess you are now going to tell him you have."

"No. Not unless you give me permission to."

"Why do you need my permission? You could just do it anyway regardless."

"Yes, but that can lead to problems down the way. Suppose I tell him, and he does something stupid to you. I'd be responsible for feeding you to him. Just bad business to go about it that way."

"I see," she said, while standing up. "I'll think about. I got your card, so I'll ring you up if I agree. Tell your cop friend he did a good job setting this whole thing up, and he can come sit down now."

I smiled as she left and Brawley came back from the bar. "Like I said, I think I'm in love."

"What you talking about? You get to go home to the princess."

Brawley laughed. "She ain't no princess; she just likes thinkin' she is. She's only a Romanov by morganatic marriage. She's really Estonian."

"How the hell did you two birds meet up, anyways?" I asked.

"I found her workin' as a pearl-diver at some slop house when I was off visiting relatives in New York. She didn't have two cents to her name or know a lick of English. But she smelled nice, even covered in all that grease."

"You damn lucky," I said, keeping the sarcasm out of my voice. "Makes me want to go out and find me a woman."

"What happened to that waitress that worked nights?"

"Gwen? She was crazy, and that's a fact. First time I took her out, she was talking of gettin' hitched."

Brawley laughed. "She'd have to be crazy to want to get married to you. Should've had your ex-wife explain that to her."

I was just a kid and my marriage lasted about three months. She was a nurse I had fooled around with until one day she said she was pregnant. This led to her father coming short of having us married at the end of a shotgun. A month in, she came clean about faking the pregnancy and I wanted to end it, but she refused. It took having her walk in on me and some nude showgirl to convince her.

"We don't keep in touch," I said, and left it at that.

CHAPTER 5

I called Bill Storm when I got to my flat with the number he had given me, but my call went unanswered. I didn't mind. It was better that he didn't respond, since I would not have provided him with any information. Not until that daughter of his gave me permission to do so.

I would've used the time to fill out a daily activity report, but seeing as the entire matter was unofficial, I satisfied my time flipping through *The Ring* magazine. I had been born a decade too early. With my prime years long gone, a black heavyweight by the name of Joe Louis finally got the chance to fight for the title. And there the champ was in a colored drawing on the cover of the magazine giving Max Schmeling a beatdown in their second fight.

I flipped through the magazine and started catching up on the rankings when the phone rang.

"Get to Congo Square soon as you can," Brawley said, and hung up.

Congo Square was located off Rampart Street in the French Quarter. The cobblestone-paved park was once the place where slaves used to get together for festivities: music, dance, trading goods, and just socializing. Large oaks and ornamentals covered the park, giving it a charming air. Except that the pleasantness wore off after sundown, when it became the ideal place for muggings, dope deals, and on occasion was a hot spot for dumping bodies.

A thick coat of mist swept down between the streets as I made the short walk to the park from my flat. The haze wasn't thick enough for me to miss the flashing of emergency lights as I came closer to the square.

Standing by one of the benches just inside the park were a dozen or so harness bulls and plainclothes detectives. I positioned myself on the outside of the crowd so they would pay little attention to me. From there, I saw all I needed to.

Bill Storm's lifeless body lay hunched over on the park bench, wearing the same clothes I saw him in earlier that morning. He looked like a characteristic transient that had fallen asleep.

There was a loud pop as one of the aluminum flashbulbs from the camera of an officer photographing the scene exploded from the humidity. One of the detectives yelled, "Get a better flash, will you! And stop takin' photos of just the stiff, he ain't goin' nowhere. I want full shots of the perimeter before it gets worked over."

Brawley spotted me soon after.

"It's not every day a big-shot hood is found dead on a park bench," he said as he walked up to me. "I recognized him right away. His mug shot been on the board at the station for as long as I can remember."

"What's the cause of death?" I asked.

"Being shot in the back of the head. Too early to tell exactly what caliber it was. I overheard the coroner, said that only his hands and jaw have frozen up, so he hasn't been dead for long. He had close to a grand and a couple of bank receipts stuffed in his money belt so that throws out any pipe dream of it being a holdup."

"Why'd you call me out here?"

"What's the point in asking me stuff you already know?" Brawley said. "You didn't tell me what you were up to tonight, and that's fine since you're all wool and a yard wide with me. I reckon I'd know soon enough, and I did. We found this stuffed in the stiff's pocket."

He handed me a folded-up parchment that had a message written in what looked like female handwriting. It simply read, "Meet me in Congo Square at 11:30 tonight. — Zella."

"Is Zella the singer at the club?" Brawley asked. I jerked a nod. "Is she his kid?"

"Why do you ask me stuff you already know?" I said.

"Confirmation is all. Figured it's the least you could do for helping you out like I did at the club."

"I assume she's your prime suspect now," I said.

Brawley shrugged. "We'll see. After her little outburst tonight, wouldn't put it past her. But I don't see her shooting her own pops in the back of the head and leaving a note with her name on it. You'd think she'd go for the family jewels first."

"It would seem more her style. Why'd homicide call you out here?"

"They wanted to know if vice knew anything about Storm being in the city, but it was news to us. It don't matter much. This investigation will last as long as it takes to process the body. Far as homicide cares, he killed two cops, and this couldn't have happened to a nicer fella."

"No, it couldn't have,"

"I hope he wasn't a client," Brawley said.

"He was not."

"Could've fooled me. The way it looks, he hired you to find his daughter. You found her, told her where he was at. She sent for him, and —" He waved toward the dead body. "And that's what we got."

"Or you could figure that he came in, wanted me to find her, I refused, because he's a criminal and say I got the impression he wanted to do harm to her, right? So I went about finding her myself to warn her off. As for her possibly killing him, as you said, the method isn't her style. Let alone leaving a note linking her to the murder. Besides, if she did, it was by her own choice, and I had nothing to do with it."

"If that's your story, stick to it. I'll keep a lid on your involvement in this unless it comes up, but don't expect me to be alibiing you."

"I won't," I said.

"I wouldn't sweat it too much. It'll go cold as soon as something more important comes through the pipe."

We spoke a bit longer before Brawley went back to the other officers who were wrapping the scene up. I watched as two officers brusquely yanked Storm's lifeless body off the bench, and dragged it toward the back of the waiting morgue wagon.

There he'd be taken to coroner's office, where he'd be put in a steel refrigerator until he could be examined.

I suppose a normal person would feel something about an old acquaintance winding up dead. I felt nothing. It was always going to end this way for him, the only surprise being it took this long. And yet even in death, Storm seemed to have a way of taking people down with him, in this case, his own daughter. I did not like the idea of having gotten her involved and in the crosshairs of the police.

A small, ghoulish crowd had gathered around the corpse. They watched as the attendants unceremoniously tossed Storm into the back of the wagon as if he was nothing more than a bag of laundry and they pulled out.

Bill Storm was on the front of the morning paper with the overglamorized headline: "Notorious Heavy Found Dead in Congo Square." The article read:

At around midnight this morning a pedestrian passing through Congo Square found the lifeless body of a man slumped over on a park bench. The police were notified, and the body was promptly identified as known New York criminal Bill Storm. The coroner's office cited the cause of death as being a gunshot, possibly a .38, to the back of the head. No known witnesses or suspects were disclosed by the police when this story made print. Storm was wanted for a kidnapping charge in Brooklyn that dated back over a decade and the death of two police officers who were killed when Storm escaped capture. Authorities did not know Storm's whereabouts until now. It is still a mystery to them where Storm had been all these years, and one that will likely not be solved anytime soon.

I pushed the paper aside, and went through the stack of mail I found wedged under my door. It was all bills, the biggest being from the Bell Company. Oh, Ma Bell, the evil madam that controlled most, if not all, phone companies, wanted her money. It took little time before I stuffed the mail and all its contents into the waiting garbage can.

After breakfast, I drove out to the coroner's office on St. Peter Street. The coroner himself, Joel Wilkins, was not a pathologist, nor did he have any medical background. He was a used-car salesman who got elected since no physician wanted the low-paying position. He ran the place the same way he ran his business: into the ground. There were many reports that he diverted the annual budget money, which should've gone to supplies and salaries, into his own pocket. This led to a pileup of bodies waiting to be examined since last summer, but little to no staff to do it. There were newspaper rumors that Wilkins was to be audited for grand larceny charges for stealing state funds.

Yet Wilkins was the type of man I liked dealing with, because no matter what his personal prejudices were, the desire to make a buck or bargain trumped it. The few dealings I had with him, I negotiated with money. Yet when I heard him grumbling about not being able to get tickets to an upcoming fight at the Coliseum, I used the few contacts I still had with the boxing world to get him a pair.

He could always be found in his office, signing death certificates or betting on the ponies and anything else that had four legs and could run.

His office, endowed with a solid wood office desk and a deep chestnut-brown filing cabinet, smelled of stale carpets and furniture polish. Wilkins ignored me as I came in. Instead, he sat behind his desk on an Old Rimu captain's chair, cradling his phone like a hophead cradled a mud pipe.

Wilkins was tall, about six foot two, and I guessed through my years of sizing opponents' actual weight, weighed around one hundred and ninety pounds, with slick black hair, sharp blue eyes, and wearing a loud blue suit.

I sat down at the executive guest chair across from his desk and waited for him to finish. When he hung up, he said, "What'd you want?"

"Come to cash in on your IOU for those tickets I scored for you."

"So you were bribing me?"

"I wouldn't bribe you, that's illegal. Getting you them tickets was me being generous."

"Well, the fight was awful. They kept clenching for all the rounds, and there was no knockout."

"You wanted tickets, I got them for you. It ain't my fault the fight was all rot. You should've paid more attention to who was being matched up. You get two out-of-shape heavies in the ring, and that's what you're gonna get."

"All right, all right, what can I get you so you can get out of here?"

"Bill Storm was brought in last night. I'd like to have a look at the autopsy report."

70

"Why, so you can sell it off to the papers?"

"I wouldn't do something that could get you in more trouble than you're already in."

"I'm not in any trouble. Those state investigators can go through my books all they want, they won't find anything. They're just trying to put the blame on me for their lack of proper funding. The real crooks are them, not me."

"If that's how you see it, I won't argue with you," I said. "Personally, I hope you stay at this job."

"Why's that?"

"I don't like you, and you don't like me. But that don't keep us from doing business."

"You're right about me not liking you," he said, slouching back in his chair and putting his hands behind his greasy hair. "They just got finished with him."

"Were you there for the autopsy?"

"No way. I don't even want to be in the same room as a dead body. They scare the hell out of me."

"You picked an odd career for someone that doesn't like seeing dead bodies."

Wilkins shrugged. "Nobody else wanted it. Wait here."

He left his office. I waited. He returned

71

with a folder and slapped it down on his desk.

"This is hot stuff, haven't even released it to the cops yet," he said. This was his salesman's way of telling me how valuable a commodity he was giving to me in exchange.

"What're the findings?" I asked.

"They pulled a .38 bullet out of his head. Safe to say, that's what did the chap in, right? But if the bullet didn't kill him, he would've died of a whole lot of things. He had a bunch of problems; kidney, liver, heart. I ain't no doctor, but he should've been dead already."

I said, "Looks like the lead put him out his misery."

"You could say that. Not a bad way to go, if you ask me."

He handed over the report. It was a standard form, broken into external and internal examination, evidence, and opinion. Wilkins was correct: under the internal section was a shopping list of problems that were discovered. Storm wasn't lying about not having long to live.

Wilkins said, "We finished here?"

I said we were. On my way out, I glanced into the examining room. Two pathologists were overseeing an assembly line of corpses.

72

The dieners worked fast to clean and prep the bodies once the pathologists were done in order to make room for the next batch of flesh. Only the sound of hammering, sawing, and laughter could be heard from inside.

I got back to my apartment in time to catch the ringing phone and found a husky female voice at the end of it which I recognized immediately.

"Is this William Fletcher?"

"Yes, it is. What can I do for you, Zella?"

There was a pause. "I called to tell you there is no point in me thinking about seeing my dad on account that he's dead."

"Yes, I know," I said.

"Read it from the papers, did you?"

"No, I was there when they were hauling him off."

"My, you get around, don't you? I suppose you also know that the police dragged me in for questioning early this morning."

"I figured they'd do as much."

"Do you know anything about this supposed note I sent telling him to meet me at that park?"

"No, I don't. I only know that you didn't write it. Unless you figured it out on your own where he was, which'd be a nifty trick, since I don't even know that."

"I didn't. I told the police that, too. I mentioned that you told me he was looking for me, but you left it up to me to let you know if I wanted to meet him or not."

"What did the police say to that?" I asked.

"Nothing. But they did have a few nasty looks when I mentioned your name. Not the most popular one with them, are you?"

"That's something I've been trying to rectify," I said. "It's bad for business when you got almost every cop in town stacked against you. But you seem to have come out of it unscathed. They let you go."

"They had to. They really didn't have anything. Anyone could have written that note, but I sure as hell didn't. What's your take on it?"

"I think it speaks for itself. The note was just an easy ploy to draw him out into the open."

"They wanted me to claim the body," she said. "But I refused. I ain't paying for that bastard's burial costs. I applied for county disposition."

"That works," I said. "I suppose that's that. Good luck with your singing and all."

"Oh, about that," she said, and went on to tell me she would be singing tonight at a new, "classier" venue a few blocks up from

74

where she had performed.

Apparently Zella and the owner had some choice words with each other that ended with her quitting. Lucky for her, she got a call from a promoter of a competing establishment in need of entertainment tonight

"Said if I do well," she continued, "I'll get more bookings with him. You best not be getting any wrong ideas; this ain't no whorehouse like the last joint."

"I'm sure it isn't," I said.

"You should come tonight if you ain't busy. Bring your girl if you have one."

"I don't have one, and even if I wanted to come, I doubt they'd accept coloreds at the door."

"I'll make sure they let you in," she said.

"What's the name of the place?"

"You'll know. It'll be the place that has my beautiful picture on it," she said with a laugh, and hung up.

For half an hour I flipped through the reverse telephone directory to get an address for the number Storm had given me. The directory was an important tool but hard to get since it was restricted mostly to telephone companies and law enforcement. Naturally, neither had any inclination to let me have one, and so I took one from the city library.

The address for the number was on Tchoupitoulas Street in the Warehouse District. Storm had to have been staying at the Sugar House Hotel. It was the only hotel there and got its name because it once was the site of a sugar mill. At one time, the Warehouse District flourished, storing everything from coffee to grain to Chiquita bananas. You wouldn't know that by looking at it today. The Depression had stopped a lot of business done on the docks and the area had since become a wasteland.

I lit a cigarette and started out the door. Twenty minutes later, I parked my lift a block away from the hotel, and took out a pair of sheepskin driving gloves, which I rarely used for actual driving, and lock picking tools from the glove compartment.

The hotel was made of the same exposed brick and steel as most old warehouses. I made my way inside and saw a fat man sitting behind the reception desk. His gluttonous figure took up most of the desk, as he hunched over an ironclad motored fan in a futile attempt to cool himself. He had thin gray hair, drooping eyes, and a fleshy face and jowls. From the bulk I could see, he looked to weigh close to three hundred pounds, and likely stood under six foot. He was dressed in a button-up white shirt, tie,

76

and suspenders, with sweat stains under his collar and armpits.

I sat at a chair in a part of the lobby that allowed me to see the large man, but at an angle where he could not see me. There I waited as he sipped on a pot of coffee about the size of a drum of oil. My patience was rewarded when he excused himself from the desk and waddled into a side door that must have been the lavatory.

I quickly went around the desk and flipped through the registry. Storm was not listed under his name, but I recognized the name "Chris Denardo" as an alias Storm used back when we were working together. The room he was listed under was 37.

On the back wall was a wooden key rack carved in the shape of a shield with numbers behind each hook scattered across it. Yet there was no key for his room. Storm must have had it on his person.

I took the stairs up to the second floor and down the hall to room 37. I put my ear to the door and tried to make out if anyone was inside. Not hearing anything, I put the driving gloves on and took out my tools.

What I was about to do was risky and something I usually avoided doing at all costs, because no matter which way you cut it, I would be illegally entering the room. If

I were to get caught, there would be no getting out of it, and losing my license would be the least of my problems.

I examined the lock and found it to be a standard pin-tumbler lock, easy to pick, like most locks. They were nothing but false security for people. The reality is, if some cat wants to get into your joint bad enough, your run-of-the-mill lock won't keep them out.

I jammed a stainless steel tension wrench into the keyhole and pushed it slightly in the direction the key would turn before inserting the pick. I raked the pick back and forth until the driving pins moved above the shear line, allowing the plug to rotate freely to where I could open the door.

I gave the hall a final look to make sure it was still empty, and stepped in, closing the door behind me. I hit the lights and found the room to be nearly empty of anything that showed someone was staying there. The wrought-iron four-poster bed was made. The maids had already cleaned the room, presumably early in the morning since all the other keys were still on the rack downstairs.

I went through a basic search of the room, but not as in-depth as some searches. I'd seen Brawley do searches where his team would tear a place apart from floorboards to ceiling, tossing the disregarded material into the center. I'd seen a woman become so distraught that she ratted her own husband out in order to spare her china set from being damaged.

I looked under the bed and hit upon a worn leather suitcase. I snapped open the locks. Inside I found a Browning HP 35 lying on top of a stack of old rags. I popped the blue steel thirteen-round magazine, and saw that no bullets were missing. The gun was clean and looked like it hadn't been recently fired.

I set the rod down and sifted through the clothes. At the bottom of the case, I found a yellow Western Union envelope with a telegram that read:

I HAVE FOUND YOUR ACHILLES HEEL STOP IT WILL RECEIVE THE SAME TREATMENT YOU BESTOWED ONTO ME STOP

I pocketed the telegram, placed the clothes and gun into the case, and slid it back under the bed. Outside the room, I made sure the door was once again locked before taking the stairs down to the lobby. The large man had resumed his position in front of the fan

at the desk, and paid me no mind as I
walked out.

CHAPTER 6

Later that evening, I headed down Bourbon, passing by the usual crowd of folks. An old Creole woman was dragging a leash behind her, although no visible animal was attached to it. Rich men who had left the wives at home were out in traditional Southern attire of bow ties, striped suits, straw hats, and walking canes to find some evening pleasure. The local former Prohibition agent, intoxicated again, was harassing fresh tourists for money.

I stumbled upon Zella Storm's photo fronting the windows of the Bourbon Street Blues Club on the corner of Bourbon and Conti Street. On the top galleries of the establishment inebriated birds were screaming down to any mildly attractive woman passing the street below to strip down to nothing but their toe polish.

The doorman spotted me. He pulled out the business card I had given to Zella.

"You William Fletcher?"

"That would be me," I said.

He jerked his head inside. "Just in time. She's about to take the stage."

I went in through the open French doors to a smoke-polluted room packed to the gills. The tables around the stage were filled with men. They were smoking cigars or drinking right out of the bottles the booze came in. Pouring shots was a waste of time for this crowd.

The waiters were as hard-boiled, plowing through the interlocking crowd like linebackers going through an offensive line.

I took my place at the congested bar, and kept myself amused by observing the barkeep deliberately overlooking me. He took orders from everyone that came up or was around, except me. I had grown so used to this kind of conduct that it had nearly developed into a sort of comedic routine.

The band of all coloreds sat on the stage cueing up their instruments. Most of the players I knew as regulars at the colored establishments I went to.

The lights weakened and the anxious crowd hollered with approval. Storm went on stage wearing another elegant black dress, and I prepared myself for a lackluster routine. To my surprise, it was even worse.

Her whiskey-burned voice was suitable but at times caustic on the ears; however, it was never her pipes that were the problem. It was her performance that came up lacking. Yet the crowd went for it. The booze probably helped, but Zella's silhouette and stunning dress were good enough distractions as any to forget her poor showmanship. It seemed Zella had found a suitable crowd.

A few minutes after her set, Zella cornered me at the bar.

"What'd you think?" she asked.

I lied. "It was solid."

"Yes, I thought so, too."

She ordered a martini and, upon getting her drink, looked at me. "You ain't drinking tonight?"

"I was going to get something, but Ethel behind the bar was too busy pretending I ain't here." I motioned to the blond cake-eater barkeep.

Her gray eyes lit up and she spun around to the bar. "Pete, come here for a minute."

Pete went to Zella like a love-struck puppy.

"Yes, ma'am?" he asked

Zella lobbed her drink in Pete's face. Momentarily stunned, he yelled, "Why'd you do that for!"

"Because you're an ass."

83

The remark sparked Pete to lunge over the bar at her. He hadn't made it clear over when I hard-pressed him back. I did not intend to push him as hard as I ended up doing. I sometimes forgot my own strength. As opposed to landing back on his feet, which I wanted to happen, he fell against the retaining wall, colliding onto the stacked alcohol jugs and martini glasses.

With fists clenched, I was ready for the oncoming throng of attacks that often ended up ensuing in situations like this. Instead, the crowd looked up at what was going on, shrugged, and went about drinking or doing whatever the hell they were doing.

"Say, let's go out to the courtyard. I could use some air," Zella said.

The back courtyard was quieter than the bar. Only a few birds stood around punching the bag with each other. One drunk had passed out on a hammock set up between two banana trees. Zella located herself near the bubbling water fountain at the center of the yard, and asked, "Butt me." I gave her a cigarette and she took a long drag and said, "Didn't think you'd make it. Is this business or a social call?"

"I went to the room your old man was staying at."

"Oh? You find anything?"

"Depends on how you look at it," I said.

I drew out the telegram and handed it to her. She gave it a hard look. "That's a nice riddle you got. What'd you think it means?"

"I think it's pretty self-explanatory. The telegraph said they found his Achilles heel. Bill Storm never valued his life much. The heel is obviously you."

"Should I be flattered?" she asked.

"I wouldn't be. I think he came here not to see you, but to warn you or protect you. Bill Storm was not someone to overreact or get scared off. So if he felt it urgent enough to come here, this person plays a rough game."

She dropped her cigarette on the ground and violently crushed what was left of it out.

"Okay, if that's how it's going to be. I want to hire you to do some protection work for me. That is, till this thing blows over or if you can get to the bottom of it. What'd you say?"

"It might be wiser to bring some law in on this."

She laughed. "Most of the cops in this town are on the take or tainted. I should know. I've seen them take bribes from club owners to look the other way. Who's to say they won't do the same for this?"

"If that's how you feel, I ain't going to

argue with you. I want to look more into this, though, and I suppose I can watch over you for a few days."

"Thought you'd come around," she said. "But I'm gonna tell it to you straight. I ain't gonna be playing no damsel in distress. I can handle myself just fine, understand? I'm just too caught up with my singing right now to be dealing with this, and you seem to know what you're doing without me gettin' into your references. Besides, having a big ape like you around might put a scare in them bums that try to give me the feel-up."

"I'm going to need some money out of you up front."

"You're sounding a bit greedy," she said.

"I ain't doing this work for charity. I'm going to need some money to cover expenses, at least a twenty-dollar retainer. If I don't use it all, I'll reimburse you the rest of it, or it can go into my fee, which is ten dollars a day."

"Ten dollars a day? You're a chiseler is what you are, mister. My plumber don't even charge that much."

"Yeah, but your plumber ain't doing protection work. If there was chance of him being shot at or having to deal with gettin' muscled up on while fixing your pipes, he'd

86

be charging the same, if not more."

"Fair enough. It's not banking hours, so I'll see about gettin' you that twenty dollars tomorrow."

"That'll be fine. When do you want me to start?"

"Tonight. I need a lift home. Pete was going to take me, but I think he's changed his mind."

Her place was on Pratt Drive along the London Avenue Canal. For most of the drive she talked about her singing, and how she was close to getting signed to a record company.

It was when we were nearing her place she said, "Oh, I forgot to tell you. I'm living with my auntie. Her name is Betty. She's nice, but a little protective. Don't worry about her though. She's just old and a bit senile these days."

I parked the bus in front of a one-half-story Creole-style cottage that had a gabled roof parallel to the street.

Inside the house, glass French doors opened to a dining room where an elderly woman sat almost in the dark. Her face was old and withered and looked like it had been worn out long before its time. Wrinkles lined her colorless skin, and her hair was the shade of ash. Thick glasses covered her tired, puffy eyelids.

"You really should stop waiting up for me," Zella said.

"Sorry, child. I get worried when you are out so late. A terrible fright comes over me."

"Stop being such a flat tire, auntie! I can handle myself fine without you being as jumpy as a cat. Besides, I got Mr. Fletcher here. He's going to be watching over me."

The old woman looked at me with either disdain or disgust, likely both.

"I don't much approve of you bringing his kind into my house," she said.

"Your house? I'm paying for this place, and it's only because you're family that I'm letting you park here. I should've told you to take it on the heel and toe the minute you started scaring off every decent boy that came calling. But I didn't."

With shaky hands, the frail woman stood up with her ivory-handled cane. "I don't have to take this from you, child. I'll pray tonight that someday some sense comes over you."

She limped out through one of the doors, which led to her room.

"She ain't so bad," Zella said. "She gets grumpy when I'm out late."

"I'm sure she's a ball during daytime hours."

"Not really, but what you gonna do? Anyway, enough of that. I'm going to fix myself for bed. It's late and I'd hate for you to drive back to wherever you live. You can sleep on the couch if you like. I'll be sure to bring you some blankets."

"Don't bother, it's a warm night," I said.

"Suit yourself."

Zella exited through one of the doors. I strolled into the drawing room. It was fitted with a black leather Chesterfield sofa in front of a polished steel and brass coffee table. On top of the quarter-inch-thick glass top were a few fashion magazines and an empty ashtray.

I fished a cigarette out of my pocket, and was midway through smoking it when the smell of lavender drew me to the door. Zella was leaning against the entryway. Her robe was open enough to reveal her black camisole and lace-trimmed tap pants.

"I'm off to bed," she said.

I crooked my head away from her and said, "I'll see about fixin' some coffee when you get up."

"That'd be grand," she said, and left.

The rest of the night was quiet, except for the chirp of various night birds and outside traffic. I lay awake smoking and looking up at the ceiling.

I struggled to think of the situation at hand. All I could focus on was Zella in her black underwear. I cursed my weakness. It didn't matter that she was the daughter of a man I came to loathe. A daughter I was helping perhaps because of some misguided belief that she could be the redemption for all the ugliness Storm had caused, and by helping her I could try to wipe my own hands clean.

Yet, tonight she showed she wanted some sort of control over me by using a tool women had used for their benefit for centuries. That being the womanly art of seduction. I did not know what her goal was in trying to do this, but I needed to refocus.

Abstaining from sexual thoughts was something I learned long ago in training camp. The old wisdom of sex weakening a fighter before he even steps into the ring had been passed on to me by my trainer. I do not think he actually believed it, but he knew it was a good way to keep his fighters out of trouble and focused on training.

I dispensed with my thoughts and was at last able to sleep. But it wasn't peaceful. I never slept peacefully. I dreamt of another man I had tried hard to forget, Hank Doyle.

Hank was a good young heavyweight who also wanted a crack at the belt. A jovial man, he was easy to like. We often sparred with each other before our fights and even went out on the town a few times. It was only a matter of time before a promoter got the idea of having us square off with the promise the winner would be in line to fight the champ.

Fighting guys you knew was common. It didn't matter if you liked a guy or not when the bell rung. That night, I showed Hank no mercy. He took a beating. I knocked him down six times in the early rounds but the referee refused to stop the fight.

By the start of the championship rounds Hank had taken a beating. Looking to end it, I staggered him with a hard jab. He managed to slip my right but I followed it up with a left. I knew before the punch hit that it would end the fight. It hit so hard it caused several women to scream as Hank fell straight back, arms and legs akimbo.

The referee did not even bother to count him out. He simply raised my hand up and the bloodthirsty crowd roared. They had gotten their money's worth.

It was not until I had removed my gloves that I saw Hank still lying in the middle of the ring, his handlers and a doctor huddled over him. They tried to revive him, to no avail, and so he was carried off on a canvas stretcher. I found out the next day that he was pronounced dead not long after he got to the hospital, from brain hemorrhaging.

The dream had me repeating the fight over and over as if it was preparing me for one day having to face him again.

I awoke early in the morning to the sight of the coffee table flipped over and the glass top split in roughly two halves.

Zella stood perched over me with an amused look on her face. "Do you want to talk about it?" she asked.

I erected myself, rubbed my eyes with my fists, and said, "I'm sorry about that. I'll pay for the damages."

"It's all jake. I never liked the table. Aunt Betty is the one that wanted it."

"I'm glad I could help you get rid of it, then," I said.

"You know, you really scared me last night. I woke up hearing this crash, and when I came in, you were tossing and turning on the couch saying stuff that wouldn't be very ladylike to repeat. I was going to try to wake you up, but was afraid you'd clock me."

"I suppose I woke your lovely aunt up as

well," I said.

"No. She takes pills. This entire house could come down around her and it wouldn't wake her. You want coffee?"

"Please."

I cleared the mess I had made, putting the smashed table out back. When I came back, Zella had coffee prepared at the dining room table.

"We can go to the bank and collect that fee you need, and then you can drop me off at the club after we're done. I'm meeting with the boys to go over our material for tonight."

"That will work. I need to get back to my flat for a bit."

"What did you dream about?" she asked.

I shrugged. "Most of the time I can't remember."

"You have a lot of anger issues, don't you?"

"I've been told that."

"I do, too. I just don't try to suppress them. Maybe that's why I sleep like a princess."

"Not all princesses sleep well."

The phone was ringing when I got to my flat. It was Brawley.

"Get over to City Hall. Emerson wants to

93

see you. You might want to bring that hotshot mouthpiece of yours, too."

Brawley was referring to Jim Prescott, who was representing me. My previous lawyer and good friend, Jean Fisher, had been murdered less than a year ago, shot coming out of court with a not-guilty verdict for a colored man accused of rape. When the American Bar Association would not allow Fisher, and any other colored, for that matter, to be a member, he joined the National Bar Association in the late twenties. It was Fisher that retained me to do legal assistant work for him, which included finding witnesses, interviewing, conducting legal research, and performing other activities Fisher did not have the time to do. He was directly responsible for my current profession. Fisher also helped push for me to get licensed.

I had been forwarded to Prescott after Fisher's murder. Prescott was gracious enough to take me on as a client, and charged me a fraction of what his normal fee would be, perhaps because Prescott had been good friends with Fisher as well, but I think it was predominantly because of the pro bono work I do for him. I had located enough key witnesses when he needed them for him to realize I would be no use to him in jail.

And it seems that's what it always came down to. You had to make yourself look irreplaceable enough with the right people. It made no difference if this was true or not, as long as they believed it to be so. Prescott knew how to work the legal system, no matter how crooked it could be, and without his counsel, I'd have been in jail over a trumped-up charge long ago.

Prescott's office was a short walking distance on a stretch of Royal Street called Balcony Row — an area that got its name from the identical houses that were built by the Company of Architects in 1832, and whose trademark was the blooming galleries that sprung out by the adjacent buildings.

I reached Prescott's place, a two-story town house converted into an office building. I climbed the interior stairs to the top floor and into the small anteroom. The room was decorated with the usual peeling wallpaper, chairs, and a dwarf coffee table with economics magazines stacked on it.

Near the door marked "Private" was a French-style mahogany writing desk, with fluted, tapered legs. Behind the desk sat a young witchy-looking woman filing her nails and ignoring the half sheet of paper coming out of her typewriter.

I placed her at being about five foot five. She had dirty blond hair, a long, narrow face, and a pointy nose. Her chin had a mole on it that looked like an engorged bug trying to burrow its way in. Her black belted shirtdress did not round out her figure much.

She was new, but that wasn't unusual. Prescott went through many secretaries because of the "extracurricular activities" he had them do.

I walked up and she looked up from her nail filing and politely asked, "Can I help you?"

I told her who I was.

"Well, Mr. Prescott ain't in at the moment. And if you're thinking of waiting for him, you'll have to do it outside. We don't want you coloreds in the waiting room scarin' clients."

"Says who?"

She said, "Says Mr. Prescott."

"He said no such thing."

"You calling me a liar?"

"I'm calling you a lot more than that."

Her nostrils flared. She was about to hiss out something when a buzzing sound coming from a glass-covered Knickerbocker Annunciator box interrupted her.

With a disarming smile I said, "Looks like your boss wants you. Tell him I stopped by and need to see him, if you know what's good for you," and left.

Back at the apartment, I paced around the room like a large cat waiting for something to nibble on. Half a mile's worth of pacing, I got the call I was waiting for.

"I scolded my secretary for the way she treated you," Prescott said. "She is really not all that bad. She has been through some rough times is all, and needs some breaking in."

"I hope you ain't the one doing the breaking," I said.

"Never mind that. What did you want to see me about?"

"I need you to go downtown. The district attorney wants me," I said.

"What the hell does he want now?"

I told Prescott the whole story. When I finished, he said, "Get down there. I'll be there as soon as I can. And don't say a thing until I get there. In fact, just leave all the talking to me."

City Hall was located on St. Charles Avenue. It was a three-story Greek Revival building made of Tuckahoe marble with

97

Ionic columns.

I waited outside the door that read "Lawrence Emerson" until Prescott arrived, gaudy as ever. He wore a double-breasted suit and nicely cut trousers. He was a handsome man, with slick black hair and cool gray-blue eyes.

Emerson was the opposite. Prescott and Emerson had gone to the same law school, but that was all they had in common. While Prescott was smooth and clever, never having a problem getting the attention of the opposite sex, Emerson's odd, studious form juxtaposed with his social ineptness made him the ultimate misfit. Emerson had hung on to Prescott's coattails through law school, hoping to get some girl's interest by mere association.

Emerson was sitting behind a spade-footed walnut desk when we arrived. He stood up upon seeing Prescott.

"Jim! I wasn't expecting you."

"I am here to see that he gets proper representation," Prescott said. "So let's get on with it."

"Very well," Emerson said, sitting back down, while we occupied the two solid Dutch oak armchairs with faux leathering on the seat and arms at the front of the desk. "We got strong claims that Mr.

Fletcher had a known criminal as a client. As you know, that can be interpreted as aiding and abetting."

"You are referring to the late Bill Storm," Prescott said.

"That is correct. The police interviewed his daughter, Miss Zella Storm. She corroborated that Mr. Fletcher was hired by her father to locate her."

"You cannot prove that. My client did not accept any payment from Storm."

"Even if that was so, he knew he was a criminal, and should have called the authorities upon Storm's arrival."

"You cannot prove he knew he was a criminal at the time. If you took it to court, I would have it tossed out as nothing but hearsay."

"I was not planning on taking it to court. I simply wanted to have a dialogue about the matter with Mr. Fletcher."

"If that were the case, you could have done it by phone or outside the office. Your intent was to bring him down here without representation and intimidate him. You got a history of doing that, Emerson. Several of my clients are victims of your bullying tactics."

"Now, let us not start mudslinging. We can be civil about this, can we not?"

"Sure we can. Is that all you got, Emerson?"

Emerson didn't say anything. He adjusted his thick cheaters, and looked down at his desk. He finally said, "Yes. That will be all for now."

"Fine. I suggest next time you get the idea of calling my client down, you do not waste his and my time."

I followed Prescott out the door, but not before Emerson asked, "Are we still on for drinks at the country club later this week?"

Not even turning around, Prescott said, "We'll see."

CHAPTER 7

For the rest of the day after leaving City Hall, I stayed with Zella. I waited as she winded down her practice session, after which we went for an early dinner before her evening performance. Zella stopped eating two hours before she had to sing. She said the digestion process would affect her voice.

Her performance went well, or at least better than I was used to. She changed the routine from the previous night, giving the people who had seen her the night before something different. The bartender happened to be friendlier toward me this time around, giving my order of coffee swift service.

Zella giggled the entire ride back to her place, but I paid little attention to what she was saying. Ecstatic, she started rambling on about how great she was tonight onstage, but I couldn't shake the lingering feeling that I'd seen the same pair of headlights drafting me every time I looked in the rearview mirror.

I shrugged it off when we got near her place and nobody was behind us. Once parked, I walked behind Zella as we headed to her door. The screeching sound of tires trying to retain a grip on the road came from up the street.

I shifted around to see a black Buick Century forcing its way toward us with the confidence of a much larger machine. In a swift motion I tackled Zella to the ground. A volley of metal came out of what looked like a radio receiver sticking out the back window. The Buick didn't slow up, but continued its acceleration once it passed us.

"Get in the house," I yelled as I advanced upon my own machine.

I roared the Ford's V-8 engine from its slumber, and tore off in the Buick's direction. I doused he headlights as the taillights of the Century came into view. The car made a U-turn on Charlotte and headed East Filmore Avenue. I permitted a number of cars to get behind them before the Century went right on Franklin Avenue.

If the driver was a hired goon, he no doubt had been instructed to take a detour until he was sure nobody was tailing him before redirecting to his primary destination.

I kept my distance with two cars in between us. It wasn't difficult to tail someone, as long as you kept the proper cover. Most people don't pay attention to who's riding behind them, but the goons I was following would be.

They stayed on Franklin before taking a right and headed down St. Claude Avenue, which turned into North Rampart. From Rampart they took Canal toward the river.

As soon as they turned toward the river, I knew where they were headed. Instead, I broke off and rerouted onto Decatur Street. I parked and watched as the Buick pulled into the New Orleans Hotel, home of the city's finest citizen, Johnnie Ranalli.

Ranalli was brought into the city by the New Orleans crime family to aid in their bootlegging operations. He later branched out on his own, running illegal gambling and prostitution rackets, among other things. When the red-light district of Storyville was shut down during the Great War, Ranalli converted much of the abandoned area into speakeasies, illegal gambling joints, and other forms of prostitution. When police raids proved to be ineffective in stopping Ranalli and other rackets in the district, the area was bulldozed to the ground.

Ranalli countered and took the gambling operations out onto the river, this time gaining enough political influence to get the police to look the other way. Yet this didn't stop a Federal racket probe being made on him that led to an indictment.

It was unclear at first what deal Ranalli made to avoid the sixty-year jail sentence he was facing. All that was known was that he and his big six muscle men had embedded themselves in the rotted hotel Ranalli had procured.

Prior to all this, Ranalli and his crew had visited the Pelican, a segregated boxing gym. When I was motivated enough, I would spar with the aspiring amateurs and up-and-comers. Ranalli came by during such a time. He had long been interested in starting his own promotional company, and offered me a job as a trainer or even a manager.

Many citizens of the city were afraid of Ranalli and there were warnings against getting into any kind of business with him. In the end, his plans never gelled. He summoned me to the hotel to tell me there wasn't a chance he could ever get it to happen. I had figured as much. I doubted I'd have taken him up on his offer even if it had come to pass.

I would again have to pay a visit to his

penthouse room above the ground floor, but not tonight. I had to get back to Zella.

Her neighbors had gathered out in the street when I arrived. I parked the car, got out, and saw that they were all looking at me with apprehension. I ignored them and walked up to Zella's house. The place wasn't as shot-up as I thought. Most of the shrapnel had hit the house next to hers, which had the hard luck of being in the proximity to where we had been standing.

Zella was sitting at the quartersawn oak dining table, listening to music over the radio. The table had claw feet and bearded heads of growling lions carved into the legs. I wondered if you were supposed to pet the thing before daring to sit next to it. I pressed my luck, and neared the primal-looking table and Zella. If Zella had been shaken up over what had happened, she didn't show it.

"You really saved my hide," she said. "I knew I done right hiring you to protect me."

"Did Aunt Betty have a heart attack?"

"She took her pills early. She's been asleep the entire time."

"I suppose the neighbors called the law," I said.

"That they did. They came by, asked a

105

bunch of stupid questions and left."

"I was hoping they'd have left someone here to watch the neighborhood for tonight. I guess I'll just stand watch instead. Do you got any rods in the house?"

"Yes, but I thought all shamuses carried their guns around," she said.

"I don't know about other shamuses, but my gun has been sitting in the closet of my place for some time now. Even though I got a permit to carry it, it doesn't stop the cops from harassing me over it. They don't like colored folk walking around with guns."

"That's a shame," she cooed. "Were you able to find out who it was that shot at us?"

"Yeah, they were working for Johnnie Ranalli."

Said Zella, "Ranalli? I heard he's a tough customer. I was told he sent a rival of his a king cake, but instead of finding a coin or a ceramic baby inside, he found his missing wife's ring finger."

"Where do people come up with this stuff?"

"You don't think it's true?" Zella asked.

"Maybe it is, maybe it ain't. Odds are, it ain't. Most of the time, it's just bunk the papers and folks make up."

"I suppose you know your stuff as far as that goes," she said. "How's about I brew you a big pot of coffee to help you stay awake tonight, and I'll see about fetchin' that gun."

"That'd be kind of you," I said.

I stood most of the night looking out the front window while sipping cups of coffee. The neighbors had disbanded an hour after I arrived. A few hours later it rained. It hadn't rained in the city in some time, and it came out of nowhere. Small, circular drops fell at first, and grew into big plump ones that bounced off the street and fragmented. Soon the road became a sheet of water, overflowing clogged drains and forming minute lakes. Then it stopped, and the sky became clear once again as if nothing had ever happened.

At close to five, a thud hit the door: the bulldog edition. I retrieved the paper off the doorstep and flipped through the pages. I found nothing of interest, except an upcoming local fight I had forgotten about. Middleweight contender Nino Lazio was to box an unknown contender out of Mexico named Antonio Medina as a tune-up fight before taking on the middleweight champ.

Morning soon came and Zella awoke. She prepared a small breakfast and had me drop her off at the club for singing practice.

I took the opportunity to go to my place, strip, shower, and sleep for a few hours. When I woke, I went to a neighboring diner where I had coffee and a po'boy before driving out for a return visit to the New Orleans Hotel.

The hotel had once been an elegant highlight of the city, but mismanagement and poor upkeep had left it a rotted, melancholy site. The exterior was made up of stone arches, gabled windows, and wrought-iron lace balconies, while the interior was constructed of marble flooring and walls that were crumbling away.

In a worse state of corrosion than the Roman Colosseum was the lobby. The walls looked like they were a slight tremor away from coming down. The floor didn't look much better. A rotted, moldy carpet ran across it like the remains of a dead animal.

The air was stale from all the windows being boarded up. A faint smell of chemical cleaners was unable to mask the sour mildew stench.

A young man stood behind a front desk that gave the impression that it'd been built from scrap wood nailed together.

"Is Ranalli in?"

"Who?"

"John Ranalli. You know, the only bird occupying this dump."

My directness didn't seem to please him. "What is this about?"

"Just tell him Mr. Fletcher wants to talk to him."

The young man gave me a firm look over, didn't like what he saw, and turned on his heels and went to an oak ring box on the back wall. The box had two rusted bells on top and receiver that looked like a tin can with string fastened to it.

He mumbled something in it, then my name, waited, then came back to me. He said, "Follow me," so I followed him up the wooden stairs with intermediate landings between the main floors. Two of Ranalli's sentinels were waiting for me as we made our way to the top level. They patted me down, said nothing, and led me into the first door along the poorly lit hallway.

The room was large with a foyer that led into the main room, which was outfitted with a wet bar, floor-to-ceiling windows, and two French doors that went to a private balcony. The interior was empty except for Ranalli, who was lying across a crimson chesterfield reading the sports page. He had dark hair that was cut short and sharp. His skin was mildly sunburned, and his raw face was becoming unsightly with age. His build was that of someone that spent his days pounding rivets in with a sledgehammer. The sleeves to his shirt stretched up to reveal two hairy forearms that were as thick as hindquarters.

"Who do you think is goin' to win to-night?" he asked, not looking up from the paper.

"The smart money will be on Lazio, but I'm thinking Medina."

"Medina? He's got a thirty-five–sixteen–two record with only fourteen knockouts!"

"Yeah, but them Mexican fighters got misleading records. They get most of their losses when they are young and thrown to the wolves."

"You better be wrong about Medina. I put my rubes on Lazio winning by a knockout in the eighth," Ranalli said, tossing the paper aside and sitting up.

I shrugged. "It could happen."

"Still workin' as a private dick?"

"That's right," I said.

"That's too bad. If things worked out, you could've done something better with your-self."

"Perhaps," I said.

"Why'd you ever quit boxing anyway? When I was visitin' that athletic club, I saw you sparring against some real pros, like

Sergio Diavolo. You weren't even tryin' and you tied him in knots so fast that his fat-boy manager came into the ring and read you the riot act."

"I reckon I was tired of the politics behind it all."

Said Ranalli, "Things would've been different had I been able to get my thing goin'. A guy like you would've had a fair shot at the title. There'd been none of that riggin' nonsense neither. People are gettin' tired of that kind of stuff goin on in the sport. Be no pullin' punches or crooked judgin'. You gotta give them fans what they want, see. That's where the real dough is. And what people want is some legit boxin'. It don't matter if you're a nigger, a kike, a coolie, long as you got the stuff in the ring, like that Brown Bomber. He's got the stuff all right."

"Yes, he sure does," I said. "But why don't we get to why I came here."

Ranalli shrugged. "Okay. Why'd you come here?"

"A couple of your birds tried to shoot up a canary I'm doin' protection for."

"How'd you know they were workin' for me?"

"Easy. They led me right to where you were jungled up at."

Said Ranalli, "That dish hire you?"

"Maybe."

"Why should I care that you're protecting her?"

"Because," I said, "you were wise to get the John Laws on your side by going stoolie. But what'd you think is going to happen now that your apes are shooting up a neighborhood?"

"They can't finger me on that," he said. "The only one that knows is you, and they'll believe a mug like me over someone like you any time of the week. Besides, every one of them bulls has got their hands stuck in somethin'. You start stackin' the iron men in front of them and they start forgetting."

"How much stacked iron will it take for them to forget the next time your hoods take a whack at her and kill a few Joe Citizens or a cop? Bribes won't matter when them boys from downtown come piling in on you."

Ranalli stood up from the settee. "Don't you be gettin' to thinkin' you're smart by coming here and telling me things I already know, get what I'm sayin'?"

"Sure, but why risk doin' the job? You're into the gambling rackets not the muscle work."

"Says you," he said. "This was a one-time

job. Just a way to get some dough out of an egg that's got to thinkin' he's got more pull than he actually does, see."

"Is that why you did a jerry-built job on the whole works?" I asked. "That kind of service may cause you problems."

"It'd only cause me problems if I didn't know how to deal with them New York hicks that walk around like they're suits workin' off Wall Street."

Ranalli wasn't the only gangster who had low opinions of the New York syndicates. Men I crossed paths with who worked for the Chicago Outfit shared similar feelings of how they ran things on the East Coast.

"See," Ranalli continued, "they're too busy playing the high-hat that they're gettin' thrown in the can because they're afraid of gettin' their manicured hands dirty covering their tracks."

"They all can't cop a plea," I said.

"Who said I copped a plea? That indictment against me went nowhere. All they got out of their probe was a bunch of accusations. They tried to accuse me of being involved in every crime that went on in this city. It might've been enough to convince a grand jury, but I had my lawyers tear into their sixty-page indictment. There wasn't nothing in it they could send me up on, and

113

they knew it. They just wanted to shut me down, and that's what they did. They got the cops here acting as my babysitter, and if I so much as organize a street game of dice, they'll send me up for racketeering."

"I'm sure you've found ways around that," I said. "Is that why you've taken up execution jobs?"

"I don't know what you're talking about."

"Who's this egg that wanted you to do the job?"

"He's nobody," Ranalli said.

"Does he got a name?"

"I don't know his real name; we just call him Valentino as a joke."

"What's the joke?"

"If you ever saw what he looks like, you'd get it."

I doubted I would ever get the chance. "So you done trying to kill off the only client I got or you going to give it another go-round?" I asked.

"We'll see if you're right about Lazio losing. I got strong dope he ain't. That's why you're comin' to the fight with me."

Zella and I stood in front of the Olympic Club on Royal between Montegut and Clouet. "Fistic Carnival" read one of the many banners strung across the gables of the four-story building.

The Olympic Club had hosted many big fights, the upcoming Sullivan-Corbett heavyweight fight being the biggest. In anticipation of the event, the club moved into the new century by wiring the place with electricity and increasing seating to ten thousand.

"I've never been to a fight before," Zella said. "But I'll tell you right now, if I get blood on my dress, I'm leaving."

I laughed. "Don't worry, I don't think we'll be that close."

"Remind me again why we're meeting up with the fella that tried to have me killed?"

"I want him to see your pretty face and go soft on you."

Zella laughed.

The rowdy crowd of fight fans coming to satisfy their blood thirst went down a block. But Ranalli had sent one of his goons to come out and fetch us to the ringside seats he had procured. I got a nasty look from Zella as soon as she noticed how close we ended up being.

From the bottom to the top balcony rows, the place was filled up with so much humanity that the building was ready to explode from the inside out. The crowd was a mingling of all classes. The men up front were formally dressed in overcoats and smocks. The farther back it went, the less respectable it got. Working men inexpensively clothed in overalls and sweat-stained white cotton undershirts with crew necks filled the air with the saturated tang of roasted peanuts, cheap cigars, and cologne that smelled like waxed linoleum.

The ring in the center of it all was bigger than the ones I liked to use. It was a boxer-friendly ring of twenty feet by twenty dimensions, which gave fighters more room to move around compared to a fifteen by fifteen "punchers ring" that gave opponents less space to run.

Around the foot-long apron corner men stood for the first of the preliminary bouts while the main trainers prepared their charges inside the ring.

"Not bad seats, eh," Ranalli said as we sat down.

"How'd you get them?"

"Bumped off couple of rich stiffs."

The comment got a scowl from Zella

"You must be Zella," Ranalli said. "Hope you ain't sore at me. If I'd known you were such a nice-looking number, I'd never sent them monkeys after you. World's full of enough ugly people, no need to start knockin' off the good-lookin' ones."

Smiling, she said, "If that's your way apologizing, I'll take it."

The first of the undercards was a mismatched fight between two lightweights. One was an offensive-minded Mexican kid, the other a defensive-minded black fighter who was more of a counterpuncher. For me, I was more of the school of thought that a good defense was a strong offense. For the most part, it worked for me except against a savvy veteran fighter who always had their bag of tricks they'd learned through the years. The Mex came right at the black fighter throwing damn near a hundred punches a round, while the black fighter did his best impersonation of a turtle by covering up with a high guard and throwing little in return.

The fight got booed by the crowd until the next fighters came into the ring. It was to be two unskilled welterweights whose idea of defense was blocking punches with their faces. Four knockdowns apiece later the fight ended in a draw.

The third undercard pitted a young light heavyweight prospect against a guy that looked like they had just pulled him off the street. He did not want to be there and showed it by getting on his bike for the entire fight. The young prospect showed his greenness by chasing after him instead of laying traps and trying to cut the ring off.

Despite the crowd's boos, it was a good learning experience for the kid. Every fighter meets an opponent that does not come to fight, but to survive and collect a paycheck. The best thing you can do is try to get them out of there in a timely fashion before they stink the joint up and your reputation along with it.

"Thank God," Zella said when the affair was over.

"Only one more fight to go, sweetheart," Ranalli said. "The big one."

The now tumultuous crowd booed Antonio Medina as he entered the ring first. Lazio made Medina and his handlers wait as he took his time getting to the ring, to a roar of the crowd's approval.

Lazio was a tall, rangy, good-looking kid nearing six foot. Medina was shorter, but more compact. His face was covered in scars from cuts he no doubt got through his years of battle.

"It ain't even going to be a fight." Ranalli chuckled. "Look how much bigger he is than that Mex."

"Size don't mean nothing if you don't know how to use it," I said.

The gong sounded, signaling the first

118

round. As I figured, Lazio did not know how to fight like the bigger man. Instead of utilizing his height and reach advantage, he gave it all up as he stomped right to Medina with the delicacy of a one-legged ballet dancer. Medina seemed more than delighted that he did not have to work to get on the inside of the bigger man, a skill he obviously lacked.

For the early rounds both stood in the middle of the ring, Medina's head resting on Lazio's chest as he hammered shots to the body. Between rounds Lazio's corner screamed at him to stop giving up his height and to box him, but Lazio ignored them. By the eighth round, he was breathing out of his mouth while his punches became more wild and loopy.

"He's finished," I said as the round closed.

"What you mean he's finished?" Ranalli demanded. "That Mex is throwing nothing but petty-patty punches to the body. Lazio is just playing around with him, he'll finish him soon. He ain't finished."

The ninth started off with the two once again meeting up in the middle of the ring, but Lazio's legs were jelly, and Medina knew it. A three-punch combo, two to the body and one to the chin, ended it, with Lazio melting into the canvas.

The crowd booed as the referee counted him out.

"Get the hell up, you bum!" Ranalli yelled.

"You can't get up when don't got no legs. All that body work paid off for Medina."

"Aw, who asked you!" he said, as he stood up from his seat and left, his goons in tow.

Zella seemed amused at the situation. "Sore loser, ain't he?"

"Yeah," I said.

"Hope he don't go taking it out on me."

"Let's hope not, but hey, you didn't get blood on you."

The succeeding days went by uneventfully. I had given Zella instructions that in public I wanted her to treat me like her hired help. This was to keep onlookers from getting suspicious at the sight of a white woman being with a colored man. She took full gain of this, and had me follow her around like her helper boy as she went into town to shop. Along the way, we'd get comments like, "Hey, looky there, it's a pair of walkin' piano keys!"

The cracks didn't deter Zella, who had a riot over dragging me to the ladies' stores, trying on clothes, and asking me if I liked this or that. She had even more of a kick going to a kink shop that had all the accessories that someone that was into heavy bondage would need.

"I could use this," she said, picking up a leather horsewhip.

"What the hell for?"

"For dirty boys that can't keep their paws to themselves," she said, giving the whip a nasty crack.

That evening after Aunt Betty had retired to bed, I sat alone on the couch as Zella went off to change into her nightwear. I smoked and thought of nothing in particular. Zella came back smelling of gin and tonic. She had dressed herself down to a sheer black nightgown with a triangular cutout where her midriff was, while the rest of it formed around her figure in a flared bias-cut skirt.

She fell into my lap and, in one swooshing backhand, knocked the lid I was wearing off my head. "It's rude wearing a hat indoors," she said.

"You been pillaging the liquor cabinet."

Her mouth opened slightly. "I . . . um . . . may have had a . . . few drinks . . . perhaps."

"You be careful with that stuff," I said.

"What do you have against drinking anyways? It ain't right for a man not to drink."

"Drinking can make a man act stupid. Do you want to see me actin' stupid?"

She scowled. "Well, when you put it that way, no, I most certainly do not."

"I reckon you wouldn't," I said.

She raked her right hand across my face. "You know, you're pretty damn ugly even after a few drinks."

"You're too kind."

"I'm sorry. That was vulgar of me to say."

"Yes, but accurate," I said. "I don't like looking at my mug neither. Why I ripped all the mirrors out of my flat."

She laughed. "It's okay. I happen to fancy your face. So many boys these days look so effeminate. There's something wrong when boys are spending more time in front of the grooming mirror than their women."

"Times are changing," I said.

She pulled at one of my damaged ears. "Got that from boxing, did you?"

I nodded. She wiggled more into my lap to the point I needed a jockstrap.

"Most gals would say it's a vulgar sport. But I got to come clean. After going and seeing it myself, it shook me up, if you know what I mean."

"Some women like seeing men beating each other to a pulp," I said.

She laughed. "Do you mind if I ask you something?"

"You might as well have asked," I said.

"Okay, I'll ask it to you now. I know that my dad was rotten, but was there anything upright about him? Anything at all?"

I scrutinized her face and saw that she very much wanted to hear something straight about her old man.

"He was a bad egg, I ain't gonna lie to you about that," I said. "But I reckon I don't have much room to talk as far as that goes. I ain't exactly I saint neither. But I will say this, he treated me the same as he would a white man. I reckon that's why I stuck it out with him as long as I did."

"That's so strange you saying that," Zella said.

"Why's that?"

"See, a person being colored never mattered to me neither. It's kinda how I got into singing. My ma would drag me to church, but I hated going. She'd get to droppin' me off, but I'd ditch, and go out on the town. One day I'm going along Bourbon and I hit a few dives. I wandered my way to the back alley of one of the joints and found a band waiting to get let in. They were coloreds, and weren't even allowed to go in through the front. It was awful. But I get to talking to them, and they invited me to come try singing for them. They're still teachin' me now."

"That's good," I said.

"Fancy that," she said. "I've talked myself dry. I'm goin' to see about fixin' me another drink. Why don't you put some music on, eh?"

She got up off me and went to siphon more booze into her. I went through her records, which were inside an oak radio cabinet and settled on Bessie Smith. I lit a cigarette as the 78 of "There'll Be a Hot Time in the Old Town Tonight" crackled over the speakers of the phonograph.

"Don't you just love her?" Zella said, stumbling back in. Her eyes were glossy and dilated.

"You keep practicing and maybe you'll sound like her someday," I said.

Her eyes expanded. "You really think so?"

"No."

She laughed. "I suppose you think my voice is too deep. I get told that a lot. That I sound too much like a man. But what am I suppose to sound like, Betty Boop or something?"

I laughed. "You couldn't sound that girlish even if you sucked on a helium balloon."

Said Zella, "Oh, hush up and dance with me, you big ugly hyena."

I danced with her for a bit, spun her around a few times, and sent her running to the bathroom, where she spent the remainder of the evening bear-hugging the toilet and vomiting.

CHAPTER 8

A week later I stepped out of my shower to a ringing phone. "The New Orleans Hotel was bombed," Brawley said. "Pineapples through the windows. Fire crew is hosing it down, but Ranalli and his men were able to escape the blast."

"Got any suspects?" I asked.

"We got a good idea who's behind it. Seems we might be havin' a gang war on our hands."

"That's good news for you. It'll give you a solid opportunity to get your name misspelled in the papers again."

"You've been really pushin' it, Fletcher," he said, and slammed the phone down so hard it made my ears ring.

I stayed in my flat most of the afternoon. Not wanting to leave the phone, I had my lunch, a reuben on rye sandwich and milk, delivered by the boy working at the nearby drugstore. My hunch was that I'd be hearing from Ranalli soon. It took into the evening for my hunch to materialize by the phone jingling.

"You hear what that hick did to my place?" Ranalli yelled, referring to Valentino.

"What'd you expect, wedgin' yourself up in a room with all them windows? You were just asking for something like that to happen. Maybe it ain't such a bad idea havin' the cops keeping you on a leash, if anything for your own protection."

"I'd be watchin' that mouth of yours," he said. "Don't you forget who you are!"

"You've got bigger things to worry about than my mouth," I said.

"I ain't worried. See, that fink thinks he's got a pair of iron balls by coming here! But it ain't balls, it's lack of brains. Any fink dumb enough to do a straight shot at me is going to be put through the grinder."

"He's here?" I said.

"Him and his apes snuck in last night. Must've took off when I told him I wasn't doing the job and not to bother askin' for a return on his dough."

"Tough break for him."

"It don't matter. Be out front in half an hour. I'm sending Jackson to get you."

"What for?" I asked.

He hung up the phone, and left me to the

127

task of figuring out what he wanted.

Thirty minutes later a Cadillac V-16 Imperial Limousine pulled to the curb on St. Ann. Jackson, the chauffeur, stepped out and opened the door.

Jackson at one time was an amateur wrestler. He was set to go to the 1936 Olympics in Berlin, before he took a trip to a bar in Tijuana and tried to outwrestle a mob of bandits that claimed they were once led by Francisco Villa, aka Pancho Villa.

Ranalli said they pulled Jackson into the back alley and took turns clobbering him across the back with two-by-fours and clubs. Jackson ended up with a broken back and was a close shave from being crippled. He joked that a person's spinal column has thirty-three vertebrae, and they ended up shattering thirty-one of his.

"How's the back?" I asked

"The back is fine. Some days it's better than others. But I suppose that's what I get for being young and dead between the ears."

"I don't reckon I ever asked why you decided to pick a fight with them Mexicans," I said.

Jackson shrugged. "I figure you get told so much by your trainers and everyone you're the best, and nobody can stop you, you start believing it. I look back now and I think I was just trying to prove something."

"You proved you can take a beating," I said.

"That ain't proving nothin'," he said. "The only reason why I'm still standing is because they put enough bolts and metal in my spine they could stretch it along the Mason-Dixon line."

"That's a lot of hardware," I said.

He agreed and drove the Cadillac V-16 engine to the Canal Street ferry, which tugged us across the mighty Mississippi to the west bank.

I did not know why Ranalli wanted me to meet up with him, but what I did know was that there was more going on than him not liking some cat named Valentino. I needed to find out if Zella still played a part in whatever Ranalli had going on.

Jackson rode the machine out onto Peter Avenue. On the corner of Sequin Street, Ranalli's Ford Model B "Deuce" V-8 sat parked. Ranalli had removed the hood, windshield, and fenders of the machine in an effort to lighten its weight.

Jackson pulled up behind the flivver as Ranalli and a skeletal man with a sunken face got out.

"One of Valentino's boys rented out the shotgun house down the way," Ranalli said.

"We gonna go surprise him and see what ol' Val's up to."

"Who's your friend?" I asked.

"He ain't nobody," Ranalli said. "If you got to call him somethin', you can just call him Tommy."

"*Tommy,* that's grand," I said. "Why'd you call me in on this?"

"You're in the lay of this when you asked me to back off that broad," he said.

"Bull. You did that because I got lucky over the outcome of a fight, but I don't think that's the real reason why you did."

"Suit yourself," Ranalli said. "You can stand out here like a boob while we go or you can walk home. I'd be careful, though. Them coppers are known to drive around this time of night ready to go to bat with them knockers they carry."

"They've never tried that monkey business on me," I said.

" 'Course they haven't. But what's it gonna be, you taggin' along with us or you goin' to be a sissy?"

"It's your ball game," I said.

"Got a rod?"

"I didn't know I was supposed to bring one."

Ranalli glanced over at Jackson. "Give him your canister. You're just waitin' in the car

130

anyway."

Jackson pulled out a nickel-plated .32 and handed it over to me. I stuffed the piece inside my waistband. I didn't like putting a gun there, not after I read up about a hood that stuffed a gat in the front of his pants only to have it go off. It came close to blowing his manhood out onto the front steps of the bank he was trying to rob.

"Tommy been out here watchin' this bird all day," Ranalli said. "Says he went to bed an hour ago. It's a cinch. You're gonna take the front, and Tommy and me will surprise this dope from the back. Any luck, he won't even be out of bed when we give him the jump."

"Then what?" I asked.

"We gonna ask him a few questions is all, and let him go back to sawin' his logs."

I didn't believe him. But I played ball and followed them until they broke off down a small pathway between the cypress shotgun house and a neighboring villa.

I went toward the front steps. Midway up to the deck, the front door went wide open and a heavyset man holding a Browning Hi-Power nine-millimeter came out.

The man was six foot, two-forty, with a brown mop of hair, slender nose, cutaway mouth, and squinting close-set eyes.

131

"Toss your iron, get on your knees, and lock your fingers behind your head!"

I did as told as he stuck the muzzle about a fraction of an inch from my forehead. I watched as he was in the motion of working the trigger when the back of his head ruptured open. He was almost able to turn around to see what shot him before he went limp. I made a quick move to the right and dodged the falling body.

Ranalli was just inside the doorway holding a .357 Magnum. I collected my tossed gun and came up the steps.

"Quick, Tommy, get this bird inside before a car comes by and sees us," Ranalli said.

I didn't think it would be possible for someone as skinny as Tommy to be able to move someone that large. Yet he managed to lift the stiff off the railing and into the house without any sign of strain. I followed behind him and Ranalli slammed the door shut.

"We got to get out of here quick. The blast from this cannon will get someone to call it in," Ranalli said.

Tommy went through the dead man's pockets and found nothing but a tin cigarette case, tobacco, and a few bills on his person.

"This clown got nothing to show for

132

himself," Ranalli said.

"He knew we were coming," I said. "Did you tip him off?"

"Why the hell would I do that? I don't have to go through that much work if I just wanted to kill a nigger. And, if I recall, I just saved your ass. So lighten up and get to searchin' this joint!"

"Search for what?" I asked.

"I dunno, maybe a map to where his boss is."

"Are you playin' dense?"

"Hey, just shut up and do as you're told!"

I didn't bother arguing it out with him. I walked through the house, which had pine floors and a twelve-foot ceiling. The rooms were built behind each other in single file like a fire drill line-up. I went through all of them and found nothing. At the utility room, I came upon drippage that was seeping out of a crack that went into the attic. A single cord hung down. I tugged it and released the upper hatch. There was a tumble and the body of a man came plummeting to the floor. He was young, in his early twenties, with blond hair and an athletic build. He'd been shot in the side of the head with a small-caliber gun. It looked like the barrel had been pressed against his skin, leaving a burn impression of it behind.

133

He was in a state of full rigor mortis, to the extent that you could probably balance him out on a chair.

Ranalli had heard the noise and he came in with Tommy.

"What the hell is this?" Ranalli asked.

I didn't say anything.

Ranalli removed his handkerchief and went through the dead man's pockets, taking out a wallet, rolling papers, tobacco, and a comb. He flipped the wallet open and whistled. "This guy been stuffin' flatfoots in his attic. His ID says he's with the PD."

Sarcastically, I said, "That's perfect."

The sound of far-off sirens came.

"We gotta get. Tommy, you and Jackson move the cars down behind us. Fletcher and I will tidy up and take the back out and cut through and meet you at Alix Street."

Tommy left, and Ranalli went through the motions of wiping all the doors and everything we touched down with his handkerchief. We went out the back and onto a side path and through people's property until we got out onto Alix. The rumbling of emergency sirens got louder as we got up to the waiting automobiles.

"Tommy, you ride back with Jackson," Ranalli said, as he got behind the wheel of the Deuce. I took the passenger seat as he revved up its flathead engine and popped it into gear.

"This bus got some power, right," Ranalli said as he steered south on Elmira Avenue. "Had a mechanic do some cylinder boring to the engine and altered the stroke of the crankshaft. This heap can now do over a hundred easy."

He proved that by getting the machine up to near eighty. There was a prowl car waiting at the corner of Eliza Street. Ranalli punched it and passed the cop at close to ninety. Ranalli had cleared through three blocks by the time the radio car pulled out and hit its lights.

"Them cops better start gettin' better machines than them Model A's," Ranalli said, making a right on Homer and then a left on Verret.

"This thing can't outrun a radio," I said. "Better hope he ain't radioing in for a roadblock and we find ourselves getting boxed in."

"Stop sweatin' it," Ranalli said. "I been doin' this song and dance with the law since Prohibition. I had to drive the big freights myself. Couldn't trust them drivers not to drink the stuff and then go ridin' their rigs up the side of a building. Only took losin' one shipment for me to put an end to it, see. You ain't gonna get good gamblin' when the joint is dry."

He made two right turns, first on Kepler and then Amelia before he made a left onto First Street. We made the ferry before it cast off. Few commuters were on board, but more important, none of them were police. With the car in idle, we sat and smoked our tobacco in quiet at first.

"Wish I didn't have to drop that mug," Ranalli said. "Was hopin' to get to the bottom of this. See what Val was plannin' by comin' here."

"Was mighty convenient that you did drop him, since you can't go about questioning a corpse," I said.

"What are you getting' at?"

"You tell me, looks to me you got it all figured out."

Ranalli grimaced. "Maybe what all them people say is right, you shines ain't made for the smart work."

"People around here say the same about wops, so what does that tell you?"

Ranalli grunted. "That's only because they're still blaming us Italians for that superintendent of police Hennessy getting killed. There ain't no shortage of wiseasses that's got to ask me 'Who killed the chief?' "

"Well, who did?"

136

"How the hell am I supposed to know? I can tell you it wasn't them nineteen Italians they arrested for it. They were framed up all the way, see, but that didn't stop them White Leaguers from lynching them in their own jail cells."

"It happens to the best of us," I said.

Ranalli said nothing. When the ferry reached the landing, he took Jackson to St. Charles and let me off.

"Be sure to reintroduce me to that harp pal of yours workin' down at the station," Ranalli said.

I slammed the door on him, and watched as he peeled up the street. I took the St. Charles streetcar to where it dropped me off at Canal on the outskirts of the Quarter. By foot, I went the rest of the way. Ducking down a secluded side street, I emptied Jackson's .32 of its bullets. I wiped it clean with my handkerchief and stuffed it into a trash can before continuing on.

An unsettling breeze passed through the night as I made my way to my flat, the kind of breeze locals say happens just before the hurricane hits.

The courtyard to my apartment was empty except for a few tenants smoking on their front balconies. They paid no attention to me. I paid no attention to them. It took longer than normal to make it up the long white rickety steps to my flat. Opening the door was no easier, but I managed. Soon as I got in, I called Zella.

"Where you been?" she demanded. "I'm paying good money for you to watch over me, and you ain't even around."

"I haven't even seen any of this good money you speak of, outside the little you gave for expenses," I said.

"Is that what this is all about?"

"No. I got caught up in something."

"Better not be a dame."

"It isn't."

"Good. I'd thrown you out on your ear if that was the reason."

"It's not."

"What was it then?"

"I'd rather not talk about it."

"Men!"

She hung up.

I awoke early and headed to the Saint-Pierre Boxing Gym on Rampart Street.

The gym was notorious for being owned by Travis Richmond, an aged veteran of the bare-knuckles days of fighting, who always took it upon himself to lecture up-and-comers on how they got it easy.

"You kids fighting with your twelve-ounce

gloves. All I see in the ring now is a couple of girls having themselves a pillow fight."

Richmond was too set in his way for it to occur to him that the use of gloves made the sport more dangerous because boxers now aimed at opponents' heads, an area bare-knuckle fighters avoided to preserve their hands, opting more for cushioned body shots.

I changed and headed straight for the leather speed bag hanging off a wooden platform that looked like a wagon wheel. I always found bag work the best way to clear my head and gather my thoughts.

The speed bag was all about rhythm and listening to the sound it made. Not too hard but a nice relaxed speed. I alternated hands in a right-right-right-left-left-left rhythm and then used both hands.

My thoughts flashed through my head at the speed of my hands. The whole works Ranalli had me involved in last night was as staged as vaudeville. He wanted me to find that dead bull up in the attic.

Ranalli's men probably were watching the place and seen that flatfoot go in the house and never come out. He brought me along because he figured I'd spill it to the cops. He probably thought it'd be mighty easy to get the cops to play along with runnin'

Valentino, or whatever the hell his real name was, out of town if he killed a cop.

I smiled and speeded up my rhythm. Ranalli was playing chess while Valentino and the rest of us were playing checkers.

I got back to my flat to a ringing phone. It was Brawley in a mood.

"We got a call last night about a gun being fired on Peter Street, and found a stiff and one of our own dead," he said.

I played dumb. "Any idea who did it?" I asked.

"One of our radio cars said he saw a make boring down a street near the scene that fit Ranalli's bucket. We already talked with him, and he was out at some whorehouse with a roomful of witnesses."

"Those aren't real legit witnesses," I said.

"Yeah, well, it's good enough for the brass. Ranalli said it must've been the number that blew up his joint. It seems to check out, since the stiff was just ID'd as some ape from Brooklyn."

"Who was the flatfoot you found dead?" I asked.

"Monroe Flori. He was some kid that was workin' a simple patrol beat until he stepped up and volunteered for the unit that was handlin' this whole mess with Ranalli."

140

"That's a bad way to go out," I said.

"Yeah," Brawley said. There was an underlying tension in his voice. "Guess what else the patrol said when he radioed in seeing Ranalli's car? Said he thought he saw a big Negro riding shotgun."

"There are a lot of big black men in this city," I said.

"You are really startin' to piss me off, Fletcher!" he growled. "Were you there last night?"

"If I give you the up and up, and you get the idea of bringing me in on it, I'll play the part everyone expects me to play, the dumb colored man that don't know nothing about nothing."

"You'll also be the dumb colored man rotting in a ten-by-ten cell, too," he said.

"Okay, then I wasn't there, and I don't know nothin'," I said.

"Goddamnit, just give me the dope! I ain't gonna bring you in unless you played a major part in it, see!"

"Fair enough," I said.

I gave him the whole yarn. When I finished, Brawley said, "And you think Ranalli set it all up?"

"Search me. He wanted me to go through the house, like he was expecting me to find something."

"It don't matter. He didn't kill Flori, the mug gettin' shoved into a drawer did."

"What do you know about a guy named Valentino?" I asked.

"Some beauty actor that all the ladies would get their undergarments wet over."

"Not that Valentino."

"Only other Valentino I've heard of is some ugly mug that runs numbers in New York."

"How'd you hear about him?" I asked.

"He tried to get Ranalli in on doing the numbers racket here, but at the time Ranalli was being brought up on racketeering charges."

"Apparently, he went after Ranalli at his joint, and the goons that killed Flori were likely workin' for him," I said.

"Then he's a dumb Dora," Brawley said. "Whoever this Valentino is, him and his mugs came waltzing into town two days ago. We found his stronghold at some run-down dive on Chartres and Poland Avenue, near the wharf. A lot of them are holed up in the building, but there are over a dozen of them spread throughout the city, taking up rooms in hotels and the likes. We're keepin' an eye on them until the chief gives the green light to run the carpetbaggers out."

"Was Flori watchin' the goon on Peter

Street?" I asked.

"Yup. Now that he's dead, I doubt the chief is goin' to have us sit around and wait anymore."

"That's what Ranalli wanted," I said.

"The hell with what Ranalli wanted! We were going to toss them out anyway. The only thing that's changed is they may not all be alive to get back to where they belong."

CHAPTER 9

It was easy to spot the building on Chartres. It was the one with two New York apes standing outside of it in heavy wool herringbone overcoats and expensive suits. The building was an old four-story Philadelphia pressed-brick apartment, now abandoned. Its cylindrical cast-iron galleries were red with rust and currently being used as a premier perching spot for the city's overpopulation of pigeons.

The two men didn't pay much attention to me until I got out of the car and stepped closer to the building.

"No vacancies, so you might as well beat it," one of them said.

"Is your boss up there?" I asked, ignoring his remark.

He didn't answer, but something caught my eye up in one of the windows. A figure looked down but quickly moved out of sight.

"I guess he is," I said. "Tell him William

Fletcher wants to see him."

"What about?" the other goon said.

"Until I speak to him myself, it's about me wanting to sell some municipal bonds, get what I'm saying?"

"I get it. A wiseass," he said. "This city is full of 'em. They don't show that kind of lip where I'm from."

"Where you from?" I asked.

"Little Italy, Manhattan," he said.

"I didn't know Little Italy was still there. I thought the Chinese sent all you dagos running to Brooklyn."

The other one said, "Hey, I know who this coon is now. He used to be the number one black heavyweight contender until he dropped off the face of the earth."

"I don't care who he is. He better shove off before I find the nearest branch and lynch him off it!"

I was about to leave when another man came out the door. "Boss wants to see him," he said.

The two guards stood with dumb looks on their faces as I followed the other man into a freight elevator with an iron roll-down cage. The makeshift shimmied and clanked all the way to the top as if it was hoisting up a full-grown elephant. It dumped us out on the top level and the man led me to one of

145

the main rooms on the floor.

There, a group of tough guys stood around a man in a deep chair. The man's grill had been burned. Long blond strands of coarse hair crept down his damaged face. In his lap was the kind of blonde you expect to be with such a crowd. She was very little, wearing a ridiculous red and black saloon girl dress with a lace-up bodice and fringe trim. It was the kind of dress worn by a woman starved for attention.

"You must be Valentino," I said.

The comment caused the man to stare at me for a few lingering moments before standing straight up, sending the blonde to the hardwood floor. "I don't like being called that. People think it's real funny when I look like this," he said.

"Sorry, it was the only name I had for you," I said.

He ignored me, and took his attention to the blonde, who was still on the floor. "Get up off the ground, woman. You must excuse Ida. She's a good woman, just not housebroken."

When Ida had gotten up off the floor, he said, "Go powder your nose, we're going to have us some man talk here."

She gave the burnt man a nasty look and stepped out.

146

"You treat your ladies well," I said.

"Better than most," he said. "I suppose you don't recognize me. Can't say I blame you, considering the circumstance."

"I don't recall ever running into you before," I said.

"Perhaps if you saw me as a fresh-faced twelve-year-old boy, it might paint a better picture."

I gave the man's disfigured face a harder look. "It does. You're that Mallon kid."

"I'm quite sure you saved my life that day when you let me go," he said. "There is no doubt that Storm, a name I've never forgotten, would've killed me when he found out my folks weren't going to pay up."

A moment of surrealness came over me as I looked at the little kid with the chubby cheeks, his facial features burned to the point he hardly looked human. The last time I saw the kid there was something not right about him and it still hadn't changed. His behavior didn't seem natural. "What happened to you?" I asked.

"You should've asked your friend Storm."

"He did that to you?"

"Are you surprised? When I was barely in my twenties, he found me in New York. He blamed me for rattin' him out to the cops and making him a fugitive. He took a blowtorch to my face and left me for dead."

"And that's when you patched yourself up and started a new life of crime, right?"

"Crime was nothing new to me," he said. "It's been part of my entire life. Where'd you think my folks got their roll from? Bootlegging at first and then they moved into other areas. After they died, I took over the operation."

"Should have stuck to your numbers, kid. You're out of your climate here. Johnnie Ranalli has got a lot of weight and the law has his back, especially after your hoods killed one of their own."

"Ranalli took my money and failed to fulfill his commitment. When I find out where he is, we're going to come to an understanding."

"Storm is dead, leave it at that," I said. "There is no profit with this hard-on you have with killing his daughter and locking horns with Ranalli."

"Not everything is about profit."

"That's what losers say," I said. "But you go right ahead and keep playing with fire. You'll see soon enough it won't just be your face that gets burned this time around."

I was to the door when he said, "I'm grateful for what you did for me. That is why I'm allowing you to walk out that door. But if you want to know what happens to people that talk to me the way you just did, then perhaps you heard of what happened to Roman Perez."

Roman Perez was a nobody blackmailer whose bloated body was recovered in a section of the old Erie Canal in New York.

The incident become big news because his sister Delphine was a popular socialite that hobnobbed with the elite, including newspaper editors, and brought a wave of attention to it and to the lack of results in finding the perpetrators.

"What'd Perez do to get that kind of treatment?" I asked.

"He made the mistake of trying to blackmail me," Mallon said.

"Must've had something big for you to do that to him," I said.

Mallon sat back down in his throne. "I guess you'll never know," was all he said.

The morning scarehead read, "THE BATTLE OF NEW ORLEANS!" The papers reported that the "battle" kicked off around two forty-five in the morning with a truck pulling up in front of the Mallon kid's stronghold. The few witnesses nearby told different accounts, ranging from it being a standard truck to a commercial one, and

149

that either the driver didn't jump out or did before it exploded, taking a large chunk of the building with it.

This was followed with a "no-holds-barred" attack on Mallon's men who were holed up in rooms around town. Their rooms were busted into and they were either shot or the room was firebombed with them still in it.

One of the men, identified as Anton Delmar, didn't want to go down so easy. He put a bullet in one intruder's head as soon as they shot the door down. Delmar's vitality was rewarded with a bullet from an M1918 BAR, shearing him in half. More than two hundred rounds were collected at the scene. Brawley told me later in the day that the boys that processed the scene said it was closer to a hundred, but the press had a habit of rounding their figures up to create more pandemonium.

Citizens and a police officer who didn't identify himself reported police involvement in the attack, but the police department spokesman denied any such participation.

Ranalli's Model B was discovered on the Metairie Road bridge that went over the Seventeenth Street Canal. Early commuters reported being blocked from traversing the bridge on both sides by a barricade of cars and heavily armed gunmen.

Ranalli's machine had been torn into by an onslaught of heavy artillery and fire-bombed. Though the paper didn't report who the attack was from, it was likely Mallon's men doing some good old-fashioned retaliation.

The car was still burning like a funeral pyre when police arrived, and a fire crew had to be assembled to put it out. A body was found behind the wheel. Officers on the scene were quoted as saying that the car and body had been set on fire with a mixture of gasoline and motor oil, common components for the homemade hand grenade.

By the time the morning extra hit the doorsteps at sunup, it was over. It was just another day outside as the news chattered over the radio waves as if a second world war had occurred.

Notwithstanding the reporters' dire attempts to incite with their perfervid coverage, most desensitized and indifferent citizens went about their daily lives as if nothing occurred. Gangsters getting murdered seemed to them a fitting end to their kind. Mayor Robert Maestri seemed to mirror the public's sympathy when he was quoted as saying, "The men who were killed were worthless members of society. They were men without religion or scruples, and a product of a foreign-based epidemic of undesirables that's plagued American society for too long. They will not be missed."

As the story progressed, details and accounts became clear. The fingers on the body in Ranalli's car were preserved enough due to fire-retardant driving gloves that an identification was made. The scorched remains were positively identified as Johnnie Ranalli. Mallon must have got word of the attack, allowing him and most of his men to escape before the building was bombed. Seven unidentified men were killed from the blast. Mallon's whereabouts at the present time were unknown.

That day, Zella stayed home. The weak sister club owner cancelled her performance and closed shop for the remainder of the day until he was sure the dust had settled. Zella said it was more like he was waiting to get his nerve back.

When I tried to call Brawley on the phone, I was told he was swamped at the station and couldn't free himself to speak. I'd have to go to him during his lunch break. Most blacks would never bother going to a police station under their own free will. It'd be the same as tossing a sacrificial lamb into a den full of starving jackals. But working with jackals was nothing new to me.

Because of all the brouhaha that had happened, everyone in the smoked-filled detective bureau ignored my presence as I entered the room.

Throughout the room, ugly, hairy, and overweight middle-aged men conferred with others and mauled stacks of paper on their disorganized desks. The desks were wedged up against each other so tight it left little walking space. Budget tightening caused the overpacking, forcing separate units to share the same work space.

The majority of them paid no attention to me; the few that did looked up from their desks to cast nasty looks. I smiled back at them.

Brawley had situated himself at the back of the room. His desk, unlike the others, was well organized and free of clutter. When I got to him, he'd been looking over a court summons while chewing on a stuffed bologna sandwich.

It took me the time to find a chair and sit down in front of the desk before he looked up. There was a bruise above his left eye.

"What the hell did she throw at you this time?" I said.

"A rolling pin. Her aim's getting better,

and I'm really starting to worry about her safety."

"What do you mean?"

"I mean," he said, "if she keeps up with this shit, I'm gonna snap on her, and it ain't gonna be pretty."

"Maybe it's time to think about cutting your losses before it gets to that. No dame is worth losing your job and going to jail, you know."

"I suppose that'd be the civil thing to do, right?" he said, raking his hands through his unruly hair. "What'd you want to talk to me about anyway?"

"I wanted to see if you got the time to find out what you can about Sal Mallon. That's Valentino's real name."

"Why's that name sound familiar?"

I said, "Mallon was the kid Bill Storm kidnapped. You must've seen it in the papers."

"That's just lovely. I'm supposed to be busting whores and going after junkies, and now you want me to stick my nose in this."

"This tip might make you look nice and pretty to your superiors. That ain't so bad, is it?"

"No, it ain't," he said. "But they're startin' to get a real good idea where this information is coming from. I shouldn't have had

154

you come here."

It would not look good for Brawley if the department started to see him as someone's puppet, especially when that someone happens to be a colored detective.

"Aw, don't worry about it," I said. "They all think I'm too dumb to actually be behind this kind of dope. If they go asking what I was doing here, tell them you brought me in for disorderly conduct."

Brawley snorted. "That'll fly real well."

There was snickering in the background. I bowed around and saw that we had attracted a small audience.

"Best get on out of here before you draw any more attention," Brawley said.

I went to leave, and found a couple of beefy men blocking my passage. They shifted to the side to allow me through, but not before one of them attempted to flip my hat off. I moved my head to the side, and made him miss by a wide margin. He didn't like that, and made out like he was going to charge me before the other man grabbed onto him.

"No sense in gettin' all worked up over a nigger," he told him.

The other man grunted and muttered something that was barely English, but I didn't stick around to try to translate.

By evening Zella stated she was hungry enough to eat a horse, so I told her I'd take her to a Cajun place that served stuff that was pretty close to a horse.

"I like your car," Zella said on the drive out. "But it doesn't seem to fit a sport like you. I could see you in a fancy roadster."

"I had one of them once. A boat tail speedster, but that was when I was making real money. Besides, me being in one of them machines would bring too much unwanted attention."

"I could see that."

We got to the restaurant, which was more like a kitchen inside a wooden shack on the outskirts of the Honey Island swamp. The outside tables were full of colored folks, while on the porch a small band played Cajun music with a fiddle, a banjo, and a mandolin.

We took a seat at one of the few empty tables and ordered sirloin steak peppered in various spices. Our food came to us fast, and Zella wasted no time cutting into it. I watched her with amusement.

"What?" she asked, seeing me looking at her. "I suppose I ain't being very ladylike."

She sat up straight in her chair, and tucked her elbows and forearms in. "That more to your liking?"

"Hey, it ain't bothering me. Just never seen a woman eat like that before."

"Well, now you have," she said, and continued cutting into her steak. We listened to the music for the rest of the meal before I asked, "What's the story with your aunt?"

"They ain't much of a story with her. I don't know that much about her. Kinda funny, but I didn't even know I had an aunt until she came to help take care of momma shortly before she died."

"Isn't that a bit odd that your ma never told you about her?"

"You didn't know my mother," she said. "The only things she talked about were the Bible and church. It was maddening when I got older. Everything I did was obscene or vulgar to her. I finally gave up trying to please her, and deliberately started wearing racy clothes and makeup just to spite her. I think that might've helped put her in the grave."

"Was that your intention?"

"Of course not," she said. "But I wasn't really sad neither when she went. We were different people, my mom and me. She was of the Old World way of thinking, and

157

me . . . well, I suppose you could call it more modern."

She was about to elaborate on that when a big hairy-chested man buzzed our table and asked Zella for a dance.

Annoyed, Zella said, "Can't you see I'm in the middle of a conversation here?"

"Who're you havin' a conversation with?"

I got up. "She's havin' it with me, so get lost."

The hairy-chested man started throwing. I ducked and blocked everything he sent at me, then feinted, which caused him to move back, throwing him off balance. As he tried to regain his footing, I threw a straight jab to the chest. It knocked the wind out of him and he fell over.

On the ground, he gasped for air as a couple of his buddies came to pick him up. They gave me ugly looks, so I gave them an even uglier look in return.

"Bigger guys don't scare you much, do they?" she asked as I sat back down.

"Naw, I fought hulks bigger than me all the time."

Said Zella, "You miss fighting, don't you?"

"Yeah, I miss it a lot. Being in the ring was the only time I ever felt free. It sounds stupid, I know, but I suppose it's kind of like when you're onstage singing."

"I see what you mean," she said. "There ain't nothin' like it. I know I ain't the best singer, but I don't care. I love doing it."

"It's not that you're a bad singer. You're not that bad at all, it's just you're not much of a performer yet. You got to do more than stand there like a statue and sing, see what I'm sayin'?"

"I do. I'd been told that before. That I should get up there, show a lot of leg, maybe hop on a piano or something. But that just ain't me."

"That ain't what I'm talking about. That kind of stuff is sideshow gimmicks for singers that can't sing well."

"I suppose. You seem to be a pretty sharp fella. Is that why you picked detective work as an alternative career?"

"Never planned on being a detective, just things kind of happened that made it so, and it turned out I was pretty good at it, I guess. Well, that's what I tell myself, at least."

"You ready to blow out of here?

"Ready whenever you are."

159

CHAPTER 10

Johnnie Ranalli's last will and testament stated that his remains were to be placed in the burial spot he had purchased in St. Louis Cemetery Number Two. This caused contention among certain citizens.

"How can that man be put in the same area as someone like Henriette DeLille, who spent her life helping the sick and dying?" one outraged woman told reporters. But the complaints fell on deaf ears, and Ranalli was laid to rest in an ornate tomb. There were rumors that the previous occupant had been put into a burial bag and pushed to the back of the vault to make room for Ranalli.

The morning following the funeral, I met up with Brawley at his house on the high grounds of the Irish Channel. The area got its name from the sizeable number of Irish workers that were brought in to help build the New Basin Canal. Upon the canal's completion, the Irish workers had firmly planted their roots in tight-knit neighborhoods in the area. Many of them now worked as longshoremen, laborers, and cops.

Brawley's house, a one-and-a-half-story raised center-hall cottage, sat on Sixth Street. As I pulled up to the house, I could see him sitting on the front porch swing. He had a single-action twelve-gauge shotgun that had about a foot cut off from the barrel propped on his knee.

"The princess said she saw a couple bad customers rolling by in a dark car. Said she's getting pre-Revolution flashbacks, so I reckon I'd rather sit out here and make her happy. Better than being in there while she's going batty."

"That's reasonable," I said. "But that's a nasty piece of hardware you got there."

"Don't I know it. The damn Germans had a diplomatic protest against these things. Said they were prohibited by the laws of war." Brawley laughed. "They just got tired of their jerry men walking into a trench and having their faces being spread across the Rhineland."

"Is that what you're hoping to do here?" I asked.

"Naw, it's all for show to please the

princess, but I don't think the neighbors are likin' it much. It's okay, though, we are thinking of moving out of this area anyway."

"Why?"

Brawley shrugged. "I figure it's that I'm getting on the princess's backside, telling her she ain't living in Russia no more, and yet here I am living in an area that's pretending it's Ireland. We got pubs every damn block, and some fool walking around playing the bagpipes and wearing a kilt."

"Ain't that a Scottish thing?" I asked.

"These guys here don't know the difference." Brawley pulled a brass double-aught buckshot shell out his pocket and jammed it into the gun. "Then there's this Irish parade every year. They always send me invitations to participate, but you ain't gonna see me dressing up as some leprechaun and dancing like a giddy little girl."

"That would be an interesting sight to see," I said.

"It ain't happening," he said. "I don't even know what the point of the parade is. If Ireland was so great, why don't they go back?"

He tossed a nine-by-fourteen-inch legal folder at me.

"That's all I could get on our Sal Mallon," he said. "Not a lot in there. Only interesting

162

thing is how his folks died. Supposedly, his old man caught the missus playing musical beds with some sailor boys, so he killed her and himself."

"You believe that?" I asked.

"Not a chance. I called over and talked to the dumb mick that was in charge of the investigation. They interviewed sonny, and he gave them the bill of goods that his old man told him about catching his old lady with the young sailor lad. I questioned why they didn't check to see if there was any blowback on pop's hands that showed he actually fired the gun, and he slammed the receiver down in my ear."

I went through the file and took down the address Mallon's family was living at during the time of the killing.

"You better not be thinkin' of wastin' your time goin' there," Brawley grunted.

"Not much else to go on. Besides, it's not like you need me to find Mallon, if he's even still in the city."

"He is. His monkey squad stuck their head out last night. They hit up Bourbon looking for a dame."

"I bet I know what dame they were looking for."

"I bet I do, too," Brawley said.

■ ■ ■ ■

By evening, I drove Storm and Aunt Betty toward the Jean Lafitte swamps, which were about twenty-fives miles out of town.

Earlier I had called in a favor from Ken JaRoux, a Cajun acquaintance that lived and worked out in the bayou. I arranged for Zella and her aunt to stay at his cabin. No one except people that lived in the swamp would be able to locate the place, and it was the safest place to be, among the gators and predators.

We got to the pier to see JaRoux already waiting for us. He was a medium size, rough-hewn figure, standing at five foot eleven, with a coarse, leathery face that been exposed too long to the severity of the sun.

"I am not going into that — that jungle," Aunt Betty protested.

"Aw — for God's sake, Auntie, get in the boat," Zella said.

JaRoux helped them with the belongings they had packed and then gently eased them into the craft.

"I'll see you in a few days," I said, and turned to JaRoux, who had walked over to me. "If the old lady gives you more lip then you can take, just feed her to the gators."

JaRoux gave a big grin. "Sure thing, boss. Been running low on bait."

I watched as he pushed the boat off, started the engine, and pointed the front of the tub into the murky waters and overgrowth that soon consumed them.

My train reservation for New York had been set for early the next morning. I drove to the Southern Railroad Terminal, a big brick building with a glass archway as the main entrance, situated at 1125 Canal Street. It had been built in 1908 by Daniel Burnham, in his trademark Renaissance Revival style.

The 4-6-2 Pacific locomotive huffed and puffed like a large beast fighting to break free of its restraints.

The crowd on the loading platform had started to board. A young man came for my luggage. He had it checked and gave it to a worker. He and his coworkers seemed proud in the way they could throw people's belongings into the luggage car.

I did not need to be told I had to go to the colored-only coach. I knew not to expect something as outrageous as equal accommodation. The coach I got segregated to was full. The five seats across that went the width of the car now held about double that number. I found my seat, or at least part of it. The other part got eaten up by a large man that needed three seats to fit him. He had a round head with sunken eyes, and so many chins that I stopped counting at three. Two meaty legs about the circumference of small oak trees supported a gut that made the Laughing Buddha look svelte.

His annoyance was poorly hidden when I told him that I'd like to have the remainder of my seat. With grunts and groans, he shifted his mass to where I was able to wedge myself in as the train started to pull off.

The conductor, an old, solidly built man that looked like the kind of gent you'd expect working at Scotland Yard came around to check tickets. I deduced that he had thrown his fair share of people off a train for not having one. It might even have been me a lifetime ago. I made sure mine was out.

The coach emptied out as the train rolled through Georgia, where many of the passengers departed, the large man next to me included. The little sleep I got was interrupted by the constant shaking and clanking of the tracks as the train passed through crossings. Yet it was the most comfortable train ride I'd ever been on. I only had to think back to days of riding the rails and fighting it out with railroad bulls — aka the cops — to realize that.

At the stop in Charlotte, I stepped out to call Brawley. I got his wife.

"Vee is not home," she said. "Zinks being good policeman better than being good husband."

"We all don't come from royalty," I said.

"Zis is vyery true."

"He may seem like a big dumb brute to you, but he tries. That's got to mean something, eh?"

There was a short pause before she said, "I vill tell him you call," and hung up.

The train pulled into the New York station around nine in the evening. I set out to the fare stand the station provided. The driver of a waiting cab obscenely prided himself in telling me he didn't take fares from colored folks. A brawny mug, he had acne scars punctured into his face, sandy whiskers, and a Yellow Cab hat pulled down to a pair of bushy eyebrows.

I was midway through yanking the man three-fourths out the window of his own cab when a young cabbie in a tweed baker's boy cap drew near.

"I'll take your fare, mister."

He led me to his Series K Checker and

drove me out to the nearest lot that would rent automobiles to coloreds.

"Jeez, mister," he said from behind the wheel. "You were about to flatten that guy back there, weren't you?"

"He just picked a bad time to start in on me."

"You must get that a lot."

"You learn to pick your battles," I said. "I doubt anyone would've cared much if he ended up getting a shiner."

"He's not part of the company. Works freelance, but the other cabbies don't like him much."

"Why's he wearing the Yellow Cab hat?"

He shrugged. "He must've stolen it from someone. I'm sure the boss wouldn't like it much if he knew he was wearing it. Our company is real decent to colored folks, we even got them as drivers."

"That's swell," I said.

"It is," he continued. "A lot of folks at first wouldn't take the car if a colored was driving, but they came around. I guess they got tired of walking. But there are still bad customers. Just the other day some unpleasant old dame left her jewels in the cab. I tracked her down, and gave them back, and guess what she gives me in return? Two lousy bits!"

168

"That sounds rough. A lot of folks would've kept the rocks and hocked them," I said.

"I thought about it. But I ain't no crook. My cousin robbed some woman of her marbles and ended up killing her. Was going to get the chair, but they made the slipup of giving him life and sent him to the Walls. Year in, him and a few inmates beat up a couple of the guards, stole their keys, and broke into the gunnery. Three days they shot it out with over a hundred of them cops that were outside the prison. It was like the damn Alamo. He got himself killed in the end. Served him right, the lousy bum."

He dropped me off, and handed me his card, which said his name was Steve Crew.

"Any time you get hassled over a fare, give me a call. I'll take you where you need to go."

"Thanks," I said.

I paid, tipped him, and went and spoke with the owner of a lot full of Detroit disasters. He rented them out mostly to traveling salesmen, charging ten cents a mile. With me, he almost asked for my left arm as collateral to rent out some busted-up Model B Ford. I drove the jalopy out to Harlem and chartered a room at one of the various flophouses, wedged between a five-cent whiskey saloon, billiard hall, and a soup kitchen.

In my room, I shadowboxed for a while to get the last remaining jitters of traveling out, and went to bed. In the midst of trying to sleep, the blinking neon sign outside annoyed me. I got up and looked out the window, going through a few cigarettes. I sat peeping out at my surroundings. There was heavy traffic on the street. Automobiles with powerful motors weaved past slower cars like utility cones. A fancy Cadillac pulled up to a bar across the way and a white man stepped out and hurried inside a bar. A few moments later, a mob of young delinquents stumbled upon the machine and wasted no time stripping the automobile of its fancy wheel covers.

The little hooligans left and the man came out with a blonde in tow. He stopped dead upon seeing what had happened to his car. Unsympathetic, the woman laughed, and kept on laughing as he chucked her into the car and tore off down the roadway.

I shut the window, lowered the drapes to block out the flashing sign, and went to bed.

I roused a few hours later and had my accustomed breakfast of grapefruit and coffee. I wanted to probe into Mallon's numbers racket, and I knew the best way to do that was to parley with the people that did the numbers.

When I lived in New York, Harlem was the epicenter of the numbers racket. It was nothing but a chump change game, and you only needed to hand over pennies to make a bet. There were profits in numbers, and it made the operators of the numbers rich men.

Things were different now. No sooner had I left, "Dutch" Schultz and the rest of his Murder Incorporated buddies muscled in on the racket. It didn't take much for Murder Inc. to cripple the colored numbers runners and take over the entire operation. Since that time, the racket broke off into factions with different syndicates running different kinds of numbers. It also cost more than pennies to place bets.

I set out and canvassed Harlem and its adjacent districts, and had chin music with every gambler, high roller, bookie, and thrill seeker I came across. My line of questioning was simple. Where could I find Sal Mallon, aka Valentino, and who were his runners. I didn't get much. The frequent retort I got was to talk to Devland, although no one could tell me how to go about locating him.

Late afternoon, I ended a pointless conversation with a snowbird that kept quivering the entire time to a tap on my shoulder.

Behind me stood a man, near six foot three, with a protracted head and broad gasoline-blue eyes. He wore a steel-colored Windsor double-breasted suit and a black derby hat. A groomed brown mustache enveloped his upper lip.

He carried a walking stick with a gold-plated brass dog head for a handle. I had seen a stick like his before, and knew it to be equipped with a .32-caliber rimfire.

"You the one that's been going around looking for Devland?" he asked.

"I might be."

"I'm Jack Stein," he said, as if I should have recognized the name. When I said nothing, he continued. "I'm looking for Devland as well. If you happen to find him, you'd be wise to let me in on it. I'm staying at the Carlyle Hotel on the Upper East Side, room three oh eight."

"I'll do that," I said, with little intention of doing that.

The man left, and I squandered the rest of the day trying to locate Devland. I tried a few ex-boxer pals I knew and local contacts that were still around, but got nothing for my trouble, so I packed it in for the night. I shot some stick at the billiard hall, and lost coin to some young ringer who claimed he hardly played, yet manipulated the table like a pro.

The next day proved to be more lucrative. I got a tip-off that Devland's alleged bookie was making his rounds on 123rd in Harlem. He'd been revealed to me by a baby-faced pubescent that favored playing the numbers over going to school.

"Dis is da cat dey always send to dis area," he said.

The kid pointed at a squat man dressed in a frayed secondhand suit. He looked like what you would get if a human mingled with a ferret, and somehow was able to engender offspring.

His nose was abnormally long and so were his ears, which stuck out from a brown hat. In his right hand was a black horsehide briefcase which he carried as if he were delivering banking credentials.

I waited for the man on the outside steps of a high-rise he had entered. A cigarette later, he came out. I took the position I always took when confronting someone. Keeping my arms raised up, I pretended I was fiddling with the pinkie ring on my left hand. I never kept my feet planted, but shifted them every few seconds.

"You do the books for Devland?" I asked.

"I know nobody of that name," he said, eluding eye contact with me.

"Are you sure? I got dope that you are working for Devland."

The man grimaced. "Look here, I work for a stock brokerage, not for no one named Devland."

"What firm?" I asked.

"Walter Jenkins and Company."

"Never heard of them, and if you are a stockbroker, you're one of the ugliest ones I've ever seen."

I wanted to get a rise out of him, and it worked. The man wrenched into his coat, and the reflective glare of a stiletto flashed into view. Given that my arms were already up and my feet not planted, I reacted quickly and grabbed the rodent's wrist before he could remove his weaponry.

"No need pulling your toothpick out. I got some dough, and want to play the numbers," I said.

"That so?" he said. "How much you got?"

I let go of his wrist and said, "A sawbuck."

The rodent didn't look amused. "Fine, I'll take it if it will get you to scram. I don't like you."

"That's understandable."

"What are your numbers?"

174

"What are the least picked ones?" I asked.

"Around here, any kind of unlucky ones."

"All right, put me down for three sixes."

He smirked. "Are you being cute, or are you some satanic loon?"

"Neither. I just figure not many be playin' them numbers, and I don't like splittin' my winnings."

He shrugged, and opened his briefcase and took the numbers down. Upon my handing the cash over to him, he gave me a receipt from the "policy book."

"I'm figuring you know how it works. It'll be in paper tomorrow under the local track scores," he said. "There will be three races goin' on today."

"That's fine," I said.

The man gave me a pungent look, shut his briefcase, and left. I let him go a few blocks before I shadowed him in my lift. He kept his hideous head down and scarcely looked behind him, which made the job of pursuing him easier. I had tailed enough people to be comfortable doing it, but still retained a healthy amount of edge. It was that edge that kept me on my feet. Like those times when your quarry turns around from the direction they were going and walks right past you, sometimes even bumping into you. I drafted far enough back from

175

the bookie while using other vehicles as concealment that it would've been hard for him to distinguish me from everyday traffic.

He got into a parked 1933 Dodge 5W Coupe, and maneuvered it onto 116th Street. I kept two cars between us as he stayed on 116th past Park Avenue, where he pulled off into a service station. Propelling past the station and into the lot next to it, I rotated the car around and parked so that it pointed back out to the main street.

I took out a street map as I waited, and got a rough outline on where he was headed. The bookie came off as a no-nonsense character, so there would be no casual driving with him. He would take the fastest route to where he was going, avoiding side streets and detours.

As I went over possible routes he'd take, the coupe pulled passed me. I allowed two cars to go before pointing the radiator of the heap back onto 116th. Keeping my distance and using the two cars as cover, I followed, paying close attention to the traffic signals ahead of me.

The light went yellow on Third Avenue after the coupe narrowly bypassed it. Two machines in front of me braked for the red, but I wasn't worried. The pedestal post light on Second Avenue had been blazing green

176

for a long cycle of time, and went amber prior to the coupe arriving at it. It looked at first like he was going to run it, but he thought twice when a sanitation truck tugged in front of him. He hit his brakes hard and stopped a hair away from being part of the truck's load.

I got a green light and stayed behind the two cars as they caught up with the bookie a little ways past Second.

The coupe stayed on 116th to the river, and took the East River Drive down to the Lower East Side and Orchard Street.

On Orchard, he steered into the back of a brick building whose sign read "Walter Jenkins & Company." I went past the building, down the road, turned around and parked kitty-corner to the building.

Orchard had not changed much. It was still a poverty-stricken slum full of immigrants fresh off the boat. Low-rise tenements made of disintegrated bricks housed many of them in rooms the size of a telephone booth.

I entered through the front of the building, and found an aged, gray-haired man sitting at a desk in the back. He wore a dress shirt with suspenders that hitched up his pants to about his armpits.

He was gawking at a nudie-girl-type book

177

but stowed it away under the business section of the daily paper as soon as he heard the entrance bell.

"I don't do business with you folks," he said to me.

"It don't look like you can afford to be picky," I said. "Are you Walter Jenkins"

"That's the name on the plaque, or can't you read?"

"I can read just fine," I said.

"Then you should've been able to read the sign at the front that says 'No Coloreds Allowed'."

"Yes, and I can also read you pretty good, too," I said. "Like I was saying, it don't look like you can be stingy as far as who you want eatin' at your table. I'm guessing that business has not been so good for you after the stock market crash. Found yourself in a lot of debt and litigation. Am I right so far?"

Jenkins didn't say anything. He just sat back in his chair and looked bored.

"I'll take that as a yes. I'll also take it as a yes that you became a subsidiary to an illegal numbers racket and you're in contact with a man named Devland."

Jenkins gave away a slight glimpse of tension in his weary face at the comment.

"I don't know anyone named Devland," he said.

Starting to lose what patience I had with him, I said, "Don't be a clown. There's been a stack of you brokers that have thrown in with the syndicates to get out of the financial jam you birds got into on Black Tuesday."

Jenkins stayed buttoned up. I might as well have had dialogue with the wall behind him.

"All right, I've wasted enough of my time on you," I said. I stepped to the back door. Jenkins didn't protest. He went back to looking at his nudie book with indifference.

I opened the back door to the "boiler room." Inside were three men. An overweight man in a suit waiting to burst at the seams, counted money over a table. The bookie I had shadowed stood just behind him. To the right of the fat man was a bruiser who looked like the Michelin Man, and like his only skill in life was giving folks the full Broderick.

"This is a restricted area," Fats said. "Lam out!"

"You Devland?" I asked.

The man elevated his head up from counting the Michigan roll he had in front of him.

"That's the colored I was telling you about," the Rodent said.

"You did an A-one job having him follow you here," the man said, and turned to me. "I'm Devland. What's this about?"

179

"I just wanted to know how the operation is running these days with Mallon going down south on you."

Taut lines intersected Devland's encompassing face. "Who the hell are you?"

I told him.

"Who're you foolin'?" he demanded. "They ain't no such thing as a colored private detective. Now, you better start telling me who you really are, and who you're workin' for!"

"Why should I tell you? I already know who you're working for," I said.

Devland's fat face flushed with redness. "I ain't workin' for nobody. Mallon is nothing more than a partner, and he's hardly even that."

"So you approved of Mallon's side project?" I asked.

"That's his business."

"Get off it. He's spending a lot of your jack on this, and with the amount of competition you have, you can't afford it. The jobbies with the deeper pockets will run you out the same way they did with the boys in Harlem."

"You seem to think you know a lot about this," Devland said.

"Why shouldn't I? I used to be chummy with a few Harlem numbers runners before the wops and the rest of you losers took it over. But that's to be expected. The only thing you boys are good at is finding easy targets and giving them a bum's rush out of their own rackets."

Devland's plump fists were clenched as he stuck his chest out like a bantam rooster. "Perhaps we do it better. Ever thought of that?"

"You seem to think so. But all of you birds draw too much attention to yourselves. You start actin' like you're big shots. But it always ends the same way, with the works blowing up in your face."

Devland grinned, the kind of Cheshire smile that something he knew but I didn't was about to ensue. Sure enough, two colossal hairy arms that were the circumference of utility poles enfolded me from behind.

Devland stepped back and retrieved his half-burning cigar from a bronze bulldog ashtray.

"Back when you could own niggers, they use to brand them. I think it's time to start doin' it again," he said. "Grab his arm, Mike."

The bruiser rumbled over to me and nearly wrenched my right arm out of its socket. I tried to resist, but the immense

181

arms that were my prison constrained me tighter.

Devland puffed on his cigar so that the tip was cherry red, and drove it into the back of my hand.

The smell of my own burning flesh and the acute pain sent me into a blind rage I had only experienced a few times in my life.

I smashed my foot into my captor's ankle with enough force that his grip weakened, and I tore free.

I went straight for Devland and aimed my fists at his chubby body. It cushioned my hands and I made short work of him as his legs buckled and he toppled down.

No sooner did he fall, Mike and the bookie rushed me. I rocked back on my feet from their blows, and hit Mike with a straight right that about sent his nose into the back of his head. He didn't drop right away, so I kept hitting his body until he did.

The bookie backed off and tried to pull out his knife again. I clubbed at him and knocked his tool out of his hand. Enraged, he swung a fist at me that missed me by about a foot. I countered it with an uppercut to his chin that could have propelled him into the ceiling.

The hairy-armed giant that had held on to me came at me fast and grappled me to the ground. He tried to use his elephant weight to crush me and then attempted to tie me up in a submission hold. He didn't figure that it's a lot easier to get out of a hold than apply one. Wiggling around to better my position, I freed up my right hand, and started pounding it on the soft spot of his face. I kept at it until he grunted and tried to tie my arm up, which left me with an opening. Escaping, I got to my feet before he could. I kicked and stomped on him until he flattened onto the floor and didn't move.

Standing over him, breathing hard, my legs and body felt shaky. I could barely stand. My vision went blurry, and when it came back, I was propped up against the retaining wall behind the building. My clothes were saturated in sweat and blood while my knuckles were raw and swollen.

I stumbled to my machine, and with shaky hands drove away. By some means, I got back to my room. I washed up, changed my clothes, and cleaned and bandaged the burn on my hand.

I sat on the bed smoking, and called the Carlyle Hotel and asked for room 308. The phone rang several times. I about hung up when a tired voice answered the line.

"Yeah?"

183

"Is this Jack Stein?" I asked.

"Who is this?"

"I'm the one that was looking for Devland. You told me to call you if I found him. You can figure that since I'm calling, that means I have."

Stein was now alert. "That so?"

"Yes. I'll give you the address if you tell me what you want with Devland."

A short pause before he said, "It's no big deal, just some business about fixed numbers."

"I think it's about more than fixed numbers, but I'll take it," I said, and gave him the address on Orchard Street.

"If this is legit, I won't forget you giving it to me."

I put the phone on the hook, filled a bucket of ice, and stuck my hands into it until the swelling went down. My knuckles had held up to the beating without fracturing primarily because they had been broken and rebroken to the point they were now nothing but calcified knobs of reinforced bone.

This kind of callus conditioning went as far back as the days when the planter would take the strongest of us younger workers and beat us into being prizefighters. It was an easy racket for planters to make side money. Every afternoon he'd have us fight each other until sundown, while he stood to the side with a switch and caned anyone that fell over from injury or exhaustion.

But them days weren't all bad. You learned to like working the ten-hour days in the fields, the same way you learned to like fighting until you were torn up raw. I didn't have any real boxing skills then, which is what caused what little looks I had to be beaten off me. It was not until Harlan Odell, a big man that used to spar with Jack Johnson, came along and taught us all he knew. I'd spend many of my days talking with him. He educated me on the science aspect of boxing, how to avoid being hit, and how there was more to the sport than just throwing fists around.

The one piece of advice I remember the most was him telling me, "You got to get out of these fields, son. Make your way to a big city or else you're going to waste your talent here until they ain't nothing left to show for it."

I took his advice, but no doubt Odell, had he lived, would be disappointed with how things worked out with me.

Brushing these recollections aside, I took my hands out of the bucket and went to bed. I slept roughly twelve hours.

CHAPTER 11

The morning paper had several articles of interest. The first article was the results from the local horse track. The numbers came from the last dollar of the pari-mutuel total of three races. First was a three-race total of \$98.33. Second was a four-race total of \$121.66, and the third eight-race total was \$166.03, making the winning number 816.

The second article read:

Four men were found shot at Walter Jenkins & Company. Police responded to a report of gunfire at the business site. They arrived to find four men who had been heavily beaten and shot in the back room of the establishment. Police suspect stockbroker Walter Jenkins may be involved, and his whereabouts are unknown at this time. Police say Jenkins has had shady dealings since his business went bankrupt after the stock market crash in 1929. There have been allegations that Jenkins was implicated in the trading of fraudulent stocks, and dealings with crime syndicates . . .

I discarded the paper and changed. My hands were sore, but after a few exercises, I got improved movement out of them.

The drive to the mansion Mallon's parents had owned before their deaths took little over an hour. The mansion was near Huntington Harbor in Long Island, and it looked like a castle. It was of French chateau design, with red-clay, tile-hipped roofs, circular towers that had conical grooves, and elongated brick chimneys.

A giant wrought-iron gate prevented me from entering the property. I parked the car on the side of the street and walked to the gate. A hundred yards just inside the entry, a tall colored man trimmed bushes with a pair of gardening shears. I yelled for him to come over.

"What do you need, mister?" he said.

"How long you been the groundskeeper here?"

"Been workin' this property going on fifteen years."

"That would mean you were around when

the Mallons lived here," I said.

The man's expression lost its warmth. "Say, what's this about, mister?"

I handed him my card.

"I can't read so good," he said.

"That's okay. It just says my name is William Fletcher, and that I'm a private detective from New Orleans."

"Orleans is a good city. Got family there. Them French folks are pretty decent to us coloreds."

"Yes, I suppose they are," I said, and changed the conversation back to the business at hand. "Did you know the Mallons well?"

"Not too well. Ruth would be the one to talk to."

"Who's Ruth?"

"Ruth was the nanny for that boy the Mallons had."

"And she's still here?" I asked.

"Sure, sure. The new folks kept most of the old help. Ruth now nannies for the new folks' two boys."

"Can I speak to Ruth?"

The man looked down at his shoes. "I suppose I can see about findin' her. But I best get back to work soon. The boss wants the place in top shape for the party he's havin' this weekend."

He unlocked the front gate and allowed me to step in.

"Wait here," he said.

I lit a cigarette and waited until he came back with an old colored woman in her eighties.

"This is the fella that wants to talk with ya," the man said.

"Sorry to bother you, ma'am," I said.

"It's all right, young man. I need the exercise. What is it you want to speak to me about?"

"Sal Mallon," I said.

Dismayed by the name, the elderly woman said, "What has that child got himself into?"

"A lot. That's why any information you can give me would be helpful."

"I don't know what I can possibly tell you, outside that the child was disturbed."

"Disturbed how?" I asked.

"He did sinful things. Things I'd hoped he'd outgrow, but I reckon he never did. There was a time I thought he'd gotten better, but he just hid it from me. When he was about fourteen I found this journal he had. It was full of awful things. He threatened to kill me if I didn't give it back, and tore up my room looking for it. He found it, but I never saw it again. I'm sure of it that he hid it somewhere."

189

"What was in it?" I asked.

"I can't say for sure. At the time my reading was not so good. I just remember certain vulgar words being in it."

"Is it okay if I have a look at the room he was staying in?"

The woman sighed. "I don't see the point. The new folks got rid of everything that was in that room."

"All the same, can I take a quick look around?"

"Oh, if you must. But you best hurry; the lady of the house will be arriving with the children soon."

I tagged along behind the woman into the castle that made me feel like I had stepped into the medieval age. She showed the way up a teakwood spiral staircase to the top floor and into one of the towers.

"This was the boy's room," Ruth said.

She was right; there was nothing in the room that showed a little boy had once occupied it. Only a reading stand and a lamp decorated the room.

"I'll be back in a moment, and then you best be going," Ruth said.

Not knowing what I was expecting to find, I tried to think how a little kid would go about hiding his secrets. Boys that did this would go about it in a detailed, elaborate way, and take pride that their parents or whomever couldn't find it. Was it worth finding? That depended on what it would be.

I made a swift assessment of the room. Not having time for scrutiny, I checked under the bed, across the floor for hidden cracks, and the walls. I searched everything but the ceiling and found nothing.

Ruth stepped back in the room and told me I had to go. I thanked her for her time and for allowing me to take a look, and showed myself out. Midway to the front gate the groundskeeper came up to me.

"I don't know if it will help, but I just remember somethin'. It wasn't too long after Ruth took the diary that the boy came up to me and said he stole it back and buried it under the harbor. Said he got the idea from all the pirate movies his dad took him to see. Told me that I best not say nothing about it if I knew what was good for me. I don't know why he bothered telling me if he was gonna be all like that."

"He just wanted someone to brag to," I said.

"I suppose."

Thanking him, I allowed him to show me out. I then bought a small shovel at a hardware store in Peter's Landing, and drove out to Huntington Harbor. Once parked, I peeled out of my suit jacket, and with shovel in hand went out under the pier.

The odds were stacked against me. If Mallon did bury something, he had probably removed it long before he left the place. My outside chance fell on him never bothering to remove his stash.

Half an hour into digging, two young lovebirds holding hands came down the pier, took one look at me and what I was doing, and backtracked the direction they came.

Forty-five minutes later I unearthed a couple bottles, an opium pipe, a shoe, and some fishing tackle. Close to calling it a day over frustration, I plodded on until I uncovered a cut plug tobacco tin box. It was approximately seven inches in length and four inches tall. The box had a painted-on picture of George Washington coated over in a brown tarnish.

I opened the rusted latch to find a gray diary inside. The pages were yellowed, and upon opening it, several aged newspaper clippings fell out. The clippings were from Mallon's kidnapping, and a follow-up article that had Bill Storm's grotesque mug shot on it.

I needed only to read the first entry in the

diary to have the once-blurry photo of Sal Mallon come into clear focus.

CHAPTER 12

I called Steve Crew to pick me up after I had dropped the heap off at the lot the next morning, and had him drive me back to the train station.

"Have a nice trip?" he asked.

"I can safely say I can go my entire life without ever steppin' foot back in this city again," I said.

Crew laughed. "Aw, it ain't that bad here. The Depression has kind of hit us hard, but things are lookin' up."

"I'm sure they are. It just ain't my city. Never was," I said.

He got me to the station in good time. I paid my fare, tipped him, and said, "You look out for yourself, kid. If you ever come to New Orleans, be sure to look me up."

"Will do, mister," he said, and pulled out.

I made my way to the platforms and picked up on a possible shadow job. He was a young kid in an oversize ten-gallon hat that made him look like a rodeo clown. I went to several different platforms and the kid bumbled around behind me trying hard not to look noticeable. *Who the hell would hire such an amateur?* I thought as I headed to my platform. I would deal with the kid during one of the stops.

The returning train looked to be much fancier than the one I came in on. Hitched to the green and gold Pacific locomotive were luxury Pullman coaches and a club car with moveable easy chairs to lounge in. Problem was, I wasn't allowed to do any kind of lounging in them.

I got put in the semi-crowded passenger car next to an old woman that kept talking to me, even when I put my hat over my head and pretended to be asleep.

The train pulled into Greensboro Southern Railway Depot in North Carolina at two a.m. The main building, made of Flemish bond brickwork with Romanesque columns, had three-story brick entry arches.

With twenty minutes to kill, I got out with the unloading passengers to stretch. No sooner had I left the main platform, the rodeo clown was behind me.

Following the crowd through main doors and into the waiting room, I detoured down an empty hall and went into the public bathroom. There, I stood by the door until I heard footsteps coming up to it. I swung the door open, and the kid tried to move back, but it was too late. I hit him with a straight jab that pushed his face back, followed by a left hook that connected with his chin. He fell over like he'd been black-jacked in both knees. I relieved him of his rod, a nickel-plated .38, and went through his wallet. His name was Michael Mooney. Also inside his wallet was a sheet of paper with my description and the flophouse I had been staying at in New York.

The only person I could think of that would have someone following me would be Jack Stein or possibly Mallon, for reasons unclear to me.

I took his boarding pass and replaced it with my business card, and stuffed Mr. Mooney into the bathroom. I got back to the platform in time for the final boarding call. On the train, I found the annoying old woman next to me would not be with me the remainder of the way. Relieved, I reclined the chair and slept until we pulled into the Birmingham Terminal Station.

The station was of Turkish-style architecture. The main building was made up of light brown brick, with a freestanding dome with ornamental glass and two towers on the north and south wings.

I used the time during the stop to visit one of the barber shops the station provided for a quick trim and shave.

"Had some business in New York, did you?" the older colored barber asked while smoothing his straight razor on a leather strap.

"Yeah, business."

I leaned back in the chair as he lathered on shaving cream with a badger-hair brush and shaved the two-day growth clean off.

"Your face got a lot of character to it," he said, as he trimmed my hair in a close-crop style similar to the kind inmates get.

"Is that a kind way of saying I ain't much to look at?" I asked.

"No, sir! You just look like you been through a lot is all. You were a prizefighter, am I right?"

"Yeah. But that was a long time ago."

"Must've been a heavyweight. Were you any good?" he asked.

"Good enough that the champ and his promoter drew the colored line on me."

"That's too bad. Lot of good fighters never got their deserved shot because of shit like that. Maybe Joe being the champ will fix that."

"Maybe."

"If you were still in your prime, how do you think you'd fare against Louis?" he asked.

I'd been asked this question many times before.

"The hell if I know. Never came across a fighter like Joe Louis. I fought a lot of Jack Dempsey types."

"Ah, brawlers."

"Or the occasional cat that liked to box but couldn't crack an egg," I said.

"I suppose you got to work with what you got. If you can't punch worth a damn you better be good in other areas."

"That's the truth."

"So what are you doing now that your punching days are over?"

"I'm just working with what I got."

I spent the following day after arriving back in Orleans updating my activity logs. Paperwork was the single most important aspect of my job and also the most grueling. I had to be as professional and thorough as possible in reports. That's because there was a good chance they'd find their way to court if I was ever served a subpoena for them — which happens.

There are some investigators that never catch on to the fact that their logs could be looked at in court. Prescott fired his lead investigator when the prosecution got hold of his case logs which contained discrediting personal side notes during an interview of Prescott's star witness.

Close to being finished with the reports, I got interrupted by Brawley taking my front door down from his pounding. I got up and let him in. I could tell he was not in a pleasant mood.

"Where the hell have you been? New York?"

I nodded.

"It turned out to be a real waste of time and dough, didn't it?"

"It would have, if I hadn't gotten a hold of this." I tossed him the diary. "You want coffee?"

He grunted yes, and pushed his way to a chair outside on the gallery. I came back with his coffee while he flipped through the pages. I sat down in a chair close by and lit my first cigarette of the day.

With a whistle he slammed the book shut. "That's some pretty intense stuff in there. Mallon wrote this?"

"Yup," I said.

"It takes all kinds, I suppose."

"That's one way of putting it," I said.

"You should know that while you were

dickin' off in New York, him and his chiselers been tearing this place down looking for that broad. They beat up the owner of the Bourbon Street Blues Club, and whattaya know, just as I thought, they were looking for that dead cop killer's little princess. We put a car out at her house, but nobody was there. The place had been ransacked, though."

"You know where Mallon is now?"

"Not yet. We bagged a few of his birds, and beat them until they lawyered up, and got some big-shot agency repping them from out of Philly. Goddamn overpaid mouthpieces!"

"Got nothing out of them?"

"Nope. Those birds would've cracked. We got a guy that's real good at makin' mugs squeal. But these days he's being busy and all dealin' with the assault charges and the ACLU."

"I can see that slowing him down," I said.

"It's all political drivel that I'd as soon wipe my ass with than deal with. These flesh pressers and shysters are just gummin' up the works on our end. It don't make a bit of difference that these apes killed a cop. We got to play ball and stand around with our thumbs up our asses and to the left until it all gets straightened out in some room full of baby-kissers."

I laughed.

"You find somethin' amusing?"

"You know better," I said, "than to come here and start telling me your sob story about how rough being a cop is. You think those boys uptown are making it rough for you, it ain't nothing compared to Jim Crow."

"I don't give a damn about no Jim Crow, or anybody for that matter, but I do give a damn about Sal Mallon. We got our own problems as is. Ever since Ranalli's death it's created a vacuum that criminals are coming out of the woodwork to fill. So we don't need no outsiders coming in and adding more trouble, understand?"

"Yeah, I understand," I said.

Three in the afternoon the phone went off. I had been rereading Mallon's diary when I took the call. To my surprise, Mallon responded on the other end with an earsplitting yell.

"Where is she, Fletcher?"

"Where is who?"

"Don't screw with me! I got boys all over that will break your face if I tell them to!"

"Aw, cut it out with the threats, will you!" I said. "By the way, how's your pal Devland doing? Heard he might be havin' problems

201

breathing these days."

"How do you know about him?"

"I reckon there's a lot of things I know about you," I said. "See, my job ain't that hard, just takes a bit of persistence."

"It ain't wise to be sticking your head in things that ain't your business —"

I cut him off. "If you're going to start bragging about what you did to Roman Perez and Johnnie Ranalli, you can put a muzzle on it. What you did ain't nothin' to gloat about, and it sure ain't anything that's going to send me running to the hills."

"Don't be so sure about that."

I laughed. "You know, you remind me of a big-headed tomato can I fought once. He talked a big game, but when it came down to gong-to-gong fighting, he couldn't even make it through the first round without getting KO'd and carried out on a stretcher. Last I heard of him, he got hit so hard he's spendin' his days eating paste and staring at walls."

"You must be dumb as a post if you think that's me," he said.

"It wouldn't be the first time I've been accused of being dumb. But let's stop square-dancing around things," I said. "Send your girl Ida over to Jackson Square within the hour. I'll meet with her, and tell her what

202

you need to know."

"Why do you want me to send Ida? You like that piece of ass or something?"

"She's ain't my type. I'm wanting her to be my go-between, see?"

A pause before he said, "You touch her, and I'll cut your fuckin' arms off," and hung up.

Ida stood on the corner of Chartres and St. Peter when I approached her forty minutes later. I had kept hidden beforehand, making sure that Mallon didn't leave anyone else behind to shadow. The precautions didn't matter. If Mallon could get a hold of my number, it'd be just as easy for him to get an address with it. Still, I didn't want to make it too easy for him.

I took Ida through the flagstone passage of Orleans Alley, which the locals called Pirate's Alley because it was believed pirates once bartered their stolen goods in the alley between the St. Louis Cathedral and the Old Spanish Governor's Mansion.

The alley poured out onto Royal Street, where we cut through to St. Ann, and up to my flat. Inside, I offered to stow the wrap she was wearing, but she refused.

"Now that you dragged me all the way here, let's get this over with. Where's this girl he wants?"

"One thing at a time," I said. "Take a seat, and let us get to know each other. Smoke?"

She shook her head at the offer and sat in the dining chair I had pulled out for her.

"Where are you from?" I asked.

"New Jersey."

"What do you do for work?"

"I don't work."

"How long you been pretending to be Mallon's girlfriend?"

This got some excitement in her. "I don't know what you mean."

"You ain't his girl. If you were, he'd have never sent you to talk with me. Mallon doesn't like dames. This diary of his proves that."

I tossed her the diary. She didn't open it.

"It's an interesting read. I happened to find the part where Mallon describes his deep feelings for Bill Storm and the perverse things he'd like him to do to him to be the most telling."

"I'm done here," she said, making a beeline toward the door.

"You don't want to talk to me, okay. I got more than I need. I think I'll hand this book over to a guy I know that works for the press. I'm sure he'd be more than giddy to run with the story. I'll make sure to have him do a name drop on you, and word things just right to make it look like you were a willing collaborator."

It was a ruse. The only person I knew from the press was a rewrite man who sat in his office all day taking down facts from field reports and cobbling them into readable stories. But the deceit seemed to work. She stood at the door, frozen. With her back to me, she said, "He paid me to pretend I was his girl, okay?"

"That's the stuff," I said. "Come on back. You sure you don't want a cigarette?"

"Yes, I would like one now."

I gave her a cigarette, lit it, then lit my own before sliding a chair beside her.

"So tell me, what's your story in this?" I asked.

"My story is I used to be a whore, but you probably knew that already."

"Not exactly, but I do now."

"Well, I was, but not a cheap one. I did the high-class jobs. My services cost a lot, and in return you more than got what you paid for. I gave my customers a night to remember."

"What really happened with Mallon and Storm the night he got his face burned off?"

"Didn't he tell you?"

"Yes, but I never bought his story that Storm went to hell and back looking for

205

him. If he were to go looking for anyone about what happened to him, it'd be me."

"Why's that?"

"You can go ask Mallon about that when you see him. Right now, I'm much more interested in hearing what you have to say."

"But they ain't much I can tell you. I don't know exactly what happened. I just know he been obsessed over this Storm fella and when he found out he was hidin' out in Boston, he did the 'come out and see me sometime' act. He didn't take no protection with him, either."

" 'Course he didn't," I muttered.

She continued. "I don't know what happened. He left to Boston and the next thing I hear he's in some hospital after a store owner found him stuffed inside his garbage bin."

I smashed my cigarette stub out. "Sounds like he had a rough night."

"That's a cruel way of putting it," she said.

"Mallon is a cruel man. You should know that, or do you just turn a blind eye to it? Why should you care, long as he's buying you expensive jewels and that fur coat you're wearing. I'm sure you got a real a kick out of him burning Johnnie Ranalli in his car, or dumping what was left of Roman Perez in the canal."

"Perez got what he deserved," she said. "He tried to blackmail Mallon."

"So he told me. What did he have on him?"

She sighed. "Perez was a weasel. He shadowed Mallon around hoping to get some dirt on him and an easy meal ticket. He got lucky and caught Mallon going to one of them male burlesque houses he'd go to from time to time. He snuck in and got a compromising photograph."

The subject made her uncomfortable so I had to push for her to continue on.

"Perez sent Mallon a copy of the photograph and Mallon went crazy. Found Perez at his flat and made him give up all the copies and the negatives before he did him in."

"He's a little flamboyant, ain't he, even when it comes to killing people," I said.

"I think the whole thing is absurd. I don't see any point on why he goes out of his way hiding who he really is. He might as well come clean about it."

I laughed. "You don't have much brains, do you."

"Excuse me?"

"It'd be suicide if he came out with it. If there is anyone viewed by folks as being lower on the totem pole than coloreds, it's homosexuals. His own men would bump

207

him off if it ever came to light."

"You have a very negative outlook on things," she said.

"I prefer to think of it as being realistic. Mallon not being able to come clean about who he is may not be right by you, but that's how things are, see. If you want to go about your life with rosy-colored glasses, that's your business. It just makes you dumber than you already are."

The remark hit its target, and caused her to get to her feet. "I don't have to take this from some . . ."

"Go ahead, finish it," I said, as I stood up to meet her.

Her mouth opened, but nothing came out. She shook her head in pure disgust and headed to the door. I didn't stop her.

"Make sure to tell him I got his diary," I said.

She hesitated as she opened the door but wasted no time slamming it behind her. I listened to the sound of her heels as they stomped down the steps, followed by a thud and a "Goddamnit!" It sounded like Ida was going to have to get herself a new pair of heels. Perhaps Mallon would be able to help her out.

CHAPTER 13

JaRoux was once again waiting at the landing when I arrived. I had phoned him earlier that I'd be accompanying him to the cabin.

There was no moon that night, making the journey through the swamp on his boat bleaker than I cared for. I could only make out the sound of snapping turtles and restless egrets. Sometimes I'd point my flash into the murk to find glowing red eyes of watching gators staring back at me.

I had fetched my Colt 1911 from its resting place in the closet before leaving. Glad to have it, I sat in the boat with a firm grip around it.

JaRoux steered the rudder through the endless maze of channels until the flickering light of the looming cabin presented itself. The lodge was made of wooden logs and elevated off the ground. It had a brick fireplace, tin roof, and a long wooden porch. It was stacked one and a half stories high, with a wooden vertical staircase in the interior that led to a small sleeping loft.

Inside, Zella busied herself boiling an oversized pot over the cast-iron stove. Aunt Betty sat in the far corner, saying nothing as we came in.

"It's about time you showed up," Zella said, looking up from her cooking. "Was beginnin' to think you went off and left us here for good."

"Why would I do that, and miss Aunt Betty's welcoming charm?"

"Be nice," she said. "She's taking it the best she can. I'll confess, she was being a pain at first, but after Mr. JaRoux threatened to feed her to his pet gator if she didn't stop the complainin', she's been nice and hush, ain't that right, Aunt Betty?"

Aunt Betty said nothing.

"What are you cooking anyways?" I asked.

"A gumbo recipe JaRoux is havin' me do."

I looked at JaRoux. "We ain't goin' to be having our food flopping all over the table, are we?"

JaRoux grinned. "Naw, it's all dead."

I helped set the French cherrywood dining table for the impending grub pile. Once the stew had finished its boiling, we wasted no time buzzing around the barrel. Aunt

210

Betty ate little, which left more for the rest of us.

A mixture of fresh shrimp and okra, the gumbo tasted a cut above the garbage you'd get at the ritzy slophouses in town.

"So, how did you two meet, anyway?" Zella asked.

JaRoux answered. "A few years back some moonshine was coming out this swamp. Was no big deal, cuz it's a common thing out here. But this stuff was pure poison. Made its way into the city and killed a few folks. So Mr. Fletcher here comes to my bait shop asking if I know anything about it. I reckon he was workin' a case on it . . ."

JaRoux was half right. It was Brawley that had asked me to look into it.

"I told him that I didn't know much, but heard rumors of an area of swamp that was being guarded by a couple armed men that meant business. So with a little exchange of money, I take him out there, and we get shot at for our troubles. But I knew another way to get out there that whoever was guarding the area didn't know about. So we come back later that night armed with some rifles, and track our way to this camp. The moonshiners were a group of roughnecks that were using old car radiators to make the shine. That's what was killing folks, it was

211

leaching out lead. We watch them for a bit, and leave, and the next evening the place gets raided by the police."

I had given Brawley a detailed map of how to get out there, along with how many men there were and who was armed. It was a cinch raid that got Brawley and his unit on the front page with a headline in boldface type that read, "Police Clearing Out the Swamp!"

We had finished the stew when a hissing sound came to the front door. Aunt Betty snapped out of her stupor and in a fright said, "You aren't bringing that monster in here again!"

"Darla ain't no monster," JaRoux said. "Don't be callin' her that neither. Don't want to make her mad, do you?"

Aunt Betty said nothing. JaRoux got up and took a wrapped chunk of raw meat out of the cooler. I trailed behind him to the front door. Waiting just beyond the doorway was Darla, who happened to be a ten-foot alligator. Her round snout hovered in the air, sniffing, while her adjacent eyes watched as we approached.

JaRoux tossed the lump of meat at her and in a vicious snap of the jaw she devoured it whole. It was a prehistoric sight.

"That's some girlfriend you got there, Ken."

"Darla's a good girl," JaRoux said. "I had her since she was just a baby. She comes and sees me all the time now. Trouble is them bull gators start getting mighty jealous. You can hear them roar sometimes when she's here."

"You best be careful," I said. "They may take one of your limbs off to impress her one of these days."

"Don't I know it," JaRoux said.

JaRoux and I went back into the cabin where Zella had cleared up the last of the dishes. For the rest of the evening I showed Zella how to play cards. I started her with a simple game, blackjack. She proved to be both an apt learner and lucky. She did what most beginners did at first, and went bust with too many cards, but a few hands into it she stayed with aces and jacks, often resulting in a "push" from JaRoux or me, who were playing dealer.

Afterwards, we set out to retire for the evening. JaRoux loaded up the potbelly stove with wood to keep the cooling shack warm for the night. Aunt Betty went to sleep in the downstairs sleeping quarters and Zella took to the upstairs loft. I slept on the floor and JaRoux did likewise on the

213

other side of the room.

The next morning I woke up early with JaRoux and we went out fishing. He caught a freshwater drum while I myself caught nothing. I hadn't gone fishing in a long while and I was in no real hurry to get back to the mainland. I wanted Mallon to sit and stew a bit in the knowledge of what I knew. This would cause him to become bolder, making his actions easier to spot. There was a flip side to it of course. A desperate man was also a more dangerous one.

In the afternoon I walked with Zella on the upland. She did most of the talking. She asked about the plants and what bird was that. At times she came off like a little girl. It made me wonder if that was who she was at her core. A little girl looking for her daddy.

I diverted such thoughts and let myself enjoy the weather. There would be fewer and fewer days like this. Winter would start rearing its ugly head soon. A ways into the hike, we rested on a log in front of a small brook.

"This reminds me," Zella said, "of the time that I let this boy take me on what I thought was a romantic picnic in the country."

"What happened?" I asked.

"He drove me out to this secluded spot in the country; it was very beautiful. I set out fixing the picnic we brought, when I turned around and saw that he had stripped down to nothing but his boots."

"I reckon you didn't like that."

"You better believe it. We got into a fantastic row, and I demanded he take me home. I was very young then and I was mostly sore because he took advantage of my naïveness to make a goat out of me. He wasn't planning on having a romantic picnic, he just wanted to tap my virginity. I learned real fast that's what all you boys want. Ain't it?"

"I guess," I said.

She gave me a quizzical look and I diverted it with a "Look there."

Zella shifted her attention to where I was pointing. Across the creek a raccoon came out of the clearing. His eyes were covered in black coloring and dark rings that went down to his bushy tail.

"He's adorable," Zella said.

I took out the Colt, which I had taken with me, and said, "Want me to see if I can shoot it?"

Horrified, she asked, "Why would I want you to do that?"

"JaRoux is real good at skinning. He could

215

maybe make you a nice scarf out of that fur."

"You're vile!"

I laughed. "Yet you don't got a problem wearing fur. Or did you think them minks donated their fur?"

"It was a gift," she protested.

"You still wear it, don't you?"

She stood up, gave me her back, and said nothing to me the entire way to the cabin. Or at dinner that evening. Afterward, me and JaRoux sat and played cards. JaRoux had brought out his bottle of dark Jamaican rum and, through much enticing on his end, I aided him in emptying its contents. I retired early while JaRoux said he would stay up and watch over the fort before retiring himself.

The alcohol-induced sleep had been swift. I dreamt of nothing except the feeling that something was hitting me in the ribs. I didn't like it, and I reached out to whatever it was in an attempt to kill it.

The sound of JaRoux shouting stirred me and I awoke to the sight of me clutching his foot. I let go and JaRoux regained his balance.

"Didn't mean to disturb you, boss. I just thought you'd want to know there is someone moving around out front."

216

I got to my feet as my back shouted out in agony from sleeping on the hard wooden floor. I retrieved my Colt from the canvas pack I'd taken and followed JaRoux to the front window.

It took a moment for my pupils to focus in on the obscurity that was just beyond the window. With no moon, only vague silhouettes could be glimpsed in the darkness.

JaRoux had placed his M-69A bolt-action .22 rifle just to the side of the sill. He now anxiously held on to it.

"You think he's still out there?" I asked.

JaRoux didn't say anything, but my inquiry got answered brusquely by a shot colliding into the window and littering both of us with shards of glass.

The shot had roused Zella and Aunt Betty from their slumber. I told them to stay down and out of sight as I took to the other side of the window. JaRoux busted out the remaining fragments of glass with the butt of his rifle and used the sill to rest the barrel on in an aiming position.

I rechecked the magazine of the Colt. It had seven bullets in the clip and one in the firing chamber. I deactivated the gun's manual safety and crouched low to the window. The second shot went straight through the window and into the back wall.

JaRoux returned fire but it was a futile attempt. Whoever it was, they were using the lack of visibility to their advantage.

I moved from the window to the back wall. There was a small hatch used to toss kindling into the house. I opened the hatch and launched myself through the narrow opening.

Once outside, I moved, crouching, through the thick underbrush of hackberries until I hid behind a cluster of greenbriers and switch cane. The spot allowed me to look to the front of the cabin from the side. With rod in hand, I waited for my quarry to show itself.

He did, by firing another discharge into the cabin. Close enough to hear the exiting blast, I sent a horde of bullets in the shooter's direction. The jungle went silent. I waited. My head throbbed and my mind was still distorted from the drinking.

I waited until my patience lapsed. Every instinct told me to wait longer, but I ignored it and set out in the direction I had shot at. A dim-witted move. No sooner had I given up my position, the sound of an inbound shot rung out, and a jagged pain penetrated my left side.

I emptied the remainder of the clip into the darkness ahead and fell to my knees.

Blood dispensed from me like a fountain of death. What a fool I'd become. Getting shot for ten dollars a day, a fee I hadn't even collected yet. There was nothing romantic about being the hero doing this job. Heroes get put into obituaries or have small post-mortem write-ups praising them, only to be forgotten about by the next edition.

I laughed at what a sucker I had become. I leaned forward from the pain and pile-drived my head into the earth.

The pain was intense, to say the least. I was now in a state of limbo. I wasn't uncon-scious anymore, but I wasn't really con-scious either. Pulled out of the dirt and dragged inside, I'd been put flat out on the table.

JaRoux lingered above me and so did Zella. Where was Aunt Betty? Didn't she want to take part in the late evening festivi-ties? JaRoux came back with a towel and had Zella pressed it down on my side. I didn't see JaRoux again for a while. He came back with an older colored man with bottle-thick glasses. The man yelled for bet-ter light as he inspected me.

He cleaned the wound thoroughly and took out a needle and thread. He stuck the tip of the needle to the flame of his lighter and started sewing me back to together like the Frankenstein monster.

The pain escalated to such a scale that I could do nothing but bite down on my own molars until I thought they would splinter. To offset the pain, I clutched on to a bottle of alcohol cleanser and sent it on its way across the room. The sound of it shattering made me feel better. At least I wasn't the only thing broken now.

When he got done sewing me up, he dressed the wound, gave Januzzi and Zella some kind of instructions, and left.

Zella tried to give me comforting looks the whole time, but it only annoyed and disgusted me. Anger swelled up. I tried to push her out of my sight, but didn't have the strength. I couldn't even look away. My body was useless, and so was I.

Chapter 14

I opened my eyes to an empty room. They must have moved me to the bed at some point. I did not have strength to even prop myself up. I could only stare up at the ceiling until the door opened and JaRoux stepped in next to me.

"Glad to see you've finally wakened, boss. You've been out of it for four days. You had a bad fever, but it's over now."

Zella came into the room as well. She tried to wash me down, saw the look on my face and thought better of it.

"Is there anything else I can do for you?" she asked.

"How about getting me a cigarette?"

When she left to do so, JaRoux smiled.

"She's been watching over you the entire time. Told her to stop fussing over you, because I know you don't like it much."

"You know me too well, Ken. Who was the man that fixed me up?" I asked.

"Oh, he's a local around here. Used to do medical work till some whites blew his clinic up. He had enough dough that he just hid out in the swamps, not wantin' to be bothered. Said you were lucky. You were hit with a rifle shot, and it was fast enough to go straight through you without hitting anything serious. Biggest worry was infection and the amount of blood you lost."

"Maybe that's why I feel two pints low about now," I said. "What happened to our unwanted visitor?"

"Oh, he's dead. You put a lot of holes in him before you went down, that's for sure. Found him hunched over in the brush just up the front."

"Where is he now?"

"I dragged him out back, but I had to get rid of the body cuz it was festerin', and Darla was startin' to take a likin' to it. Gators don't normally like human meat, but if it rots out enough they might. I tethered the body to a chunk of wood, took him out in the boat, and tossed the body in some deep water. I don't think it'll float back up. If it does, don't matter much out here. Folks here find bodies all the time, and some joke they cut them up and use it as bait."

"Any idea who he was?" I asked.

"I recognized him soon as I saw him. His

name was Delmon Porter. He's a poacher that tries to sell off his illegal goods, but no one here dumb enough to do dealings with him."

"He probably knew that Zella was here and that Mallon was goin' through town lookin' for her. I bet his plan was to come here and get her and sell her off to him."

"What I was thinkin'," JaRoux said. "He got what was comin' to him."

"I suppose," I said.

Zella arrived with the cigarette. "Sorry took so long gettin' you your cigarette. Aunt Betty was fussing again and I had to set her straight."

"That's okay. Setting Aunt Betty straight takes priority," I said as she handed me the cigarette and lit it.

"How're you feeling?" she asked.

"Weak."

"Are you hungry? Dinner is nearly ready."

"Yes, I think some grub would do me some good. But you need to stop with this pampering. I'll live. Besides, if anyone needs it, it's Aunt Betty."

"She does not. She thinks she does, but she's perfectly able bodied to do things herself," Zella said. "And don't tell me what I should or shouldn't be doing. Smoke your cigarette and hush up. You're no good to me laying there as weak as you are and I ain't paying good money for an invalid."

I didn't have the strength to argue with her. Even if I did, I doubt I would have won.

Two days later, I could walk under my own steam. JaRoux made me a cane out of an etched piece of cypress. With cane in hand, I walked around the shack then outside to rid myself of the nausea.

JaRoux had organized a group of nearby Cajun friends to watch over the cottage for the next few days. A few of them were introduced to me: Severin Granger, a long-limbed fella that didn't know a lick of English; Henri Louviere, a fleshy jovial character that had a hook for a right hand; and Don Breaux, who sat in the corner for most of the meeting whittling on a stick with a bowie knife that had a handle carved out of bone.

Zella gave me much strife upon hearing that I was leaving, which puzzled me. The morning JaRoux and me were to set out to the mainland, Zella advanced on me. She bludgeoned her lips into my face, while brandishing her claws into the back of my flesh, leaving slight battle scars. A real wildcat, she was.

It was over as soon as it happened. She

pushed me away and said, "You best get on the boat," and walked back toward the cabin.

JaRoux shook his head as we set off. "That the best you can do? A beautiful woman gives you a kiss and all you can do is stand there like a damn fool."

"She caught me off guard is all," I said.

"Sure, she did."

"Why don't you just shut up and steer the boat!"

"Sure thing, boss," he said, still smiling.

It was not that I did not find Zella alluring, for she most certainly was. Yet I still clung to the belief that she was a beauty that came from ugliness and did not need to be tainted by the likes of me.

At the landing, I reclaimed my automobile from where it was hidden away in JaRoux's shed and drove it to my apartment. I parked the machine in the garage and the attendant/handyman, who went by Ralph LaRue, approached me.

"Evening, sir, boy, am I mighty glad I caught you when I did. A couple of bad customers came in yesterday lookin' for you. They haven't left, and I reckon they up in your place now."

"What do they look like?" I asked.

"They ain't from around here, that's for

sure. Got expensive overcoats and clothes, and they talk real fast."

I thanked Ralph and tipped him. I opened the trunk to my car, where I rummaged around for a crate of tear gas. I got a hold of the stuff when a colored used-book store owner found a small army's worth of illegal weapons inside his outside trash vault. He did not want the police finding the weapons in his place of business, in fear it would scare off what little business he had. So for a nice fee, I more than happily relocated the weapons to the bottom of the mighty Mississippi, after confiscating the tear gas and a few other toys for myself.

I looked into where the arsenal came from, and learned that another used-book store owner just up the street was selling illegal weapons on the side. It seems that he got a tip the police were about to raid him and must've thought it'd be a hoot to dump the stuff off on his colored competitor.

By the time the police did show up to search his business, the store owner redirected them to my client by telling them it was my client that was in fact selling the weapons, and that he'd seen him stashing them outside in his garbage vault.

Luckily, when the police got there, the weapons had been removed, by me, but that didn't stop the police from handcuffing my client in front of his customers, taking him down to the station, and detaining him for a day.

I took one of the tube canisters out, and walked out to Royal. From the street, I glanced up into my own gallery. The inside was dark, but that didn't mean anything. I pulled the fuse and sent the canister through the window. It took but a few seconds for the sound of yelling and stuff being knocked over to reach down into the street.

I rushed back through the main entrance gate and into the courtyard in time to see my front door ajar and two big men faltering out of it. When I saw their mugs, I recognized them as Buzz Martin, aka The Saw, and Tommy O'Cahan.

O'Cahan was a block of a man, with a raw jaw and dark slits for eyes. The last I heard of him was reading in the paper that he was serving ten to thirty for an armed robbery charge. He and a few other grafters tried to bust into a New York City bank. It was a well thought-out caper, except for the timing. The execution of the crime was around noon on a Friday. It just happened that the building was full of cops from the local precinct that had taken their lunch break to deposit their weekly paychecks.

227

Martin, a colossal slab of meat, was doing muscle work around the same time Storm and I were. Now, however, age had set in on him. His muscles were starting to go soft, and his unbaked face looked like dough that had lost its form.

He was working for a narcotics syndicate that was fronting as a pharmaceutical agency. The syndicate was gutted out by the police when they got so certain that they had paid off everyone that was potent enough to shut them down that they started putting wooden overcoats on undercover narcotics agents.

Martin got his alias from his notoriety for hacking off limbs of hopheads that didn't pony up. Or maybe he just made the nickname up himself.

He dressed in a suit that had the appearance of not having been pressed in a while and a pair of immaculate galoshes.

They were both slashing at their eyes with the sleeves of their coats. I pulled the .45 out from my waistband and met them at the bottom of the stairs.

"If Mallon wants to talk to me, he can call me during regular hours. And next time you birds get to thinkin' about bustin' into my flat, just remember there's more than tear gas I can toss through them windows."

The reply I got back from them? A lot of blasphemy and threats. Nothing original, and mild compared to the vulgarity I'd get at a weigh-in when I squared off against a white opponent. Watching them leave, I thought about shadowing them. I resolved that it would be a waste since these men were good enough to expect a tail job.

I took a handkerchief from my coat pocket, smothered my face, and went up into my room. There I tossed the empty canister in the outside trash bin and examined the front door lock. An easy pin and tumbler lock to pick for someone that knew what they were doing. A pick and a flathead screwdriver as a tension wrench were all that were required. Without Jenkins's warning, I'd have never known the place had been broken into. I would've walked right in on their ambush.

When I turned the rest of the lights on, I came upon a disturbing sight. Carved into the wall above my couch were the words "ALL NIGGERS DIE!" I ignored the fumes and stood and stared at the vandalism. I kept staring. I couldn't look away. Hearing such things out in the street or in public was one thing, but having it mounted inside my own home was another. Anger came to me. I tried to control it. Losing my head was not the answer. Experience taught me that. I released my clenched hands, and looked away.

Switching the fan on, I left my apartment with the door open. I asked Jenkins to watch the place as I strode my way to a nearby diner and used the phone to ring up Brawley.

His Russian princess wife answered the call in an unpleasant mood before she handed the phone off to him.

"You are breaking the rules, Fletcher," he grumbled.

"How so?"

"When a colored isn't heard from in a week, around here, it means they are dead. You don't sound very dead to me."

"A few inches in the wrong direction and I might've been. What's been happening?"

"The usual. Mallon's heavies are running around town like they own the place, looking for that dame and us having to sit around looking like we don't know our asses from our elbows."

"Have you been able to locate where Mallon is?" I asked.

"Nope. We can't even drag his boyfriends in for questioning. We try tailing them, but they go in circles like it's a merry-go-round. We had a good tail that showed promise, followed one of their cars out on River Road, but lost them in all that country."

I hung up after we finished and went back to my place. The fumes were still too strong to occupy the place without being irritated by the toxin, nor did I want to sleep there until I had the words on the wall removed. Ralph offered me a cot in the back service room, and there I slept next to the thudding washing machine until early the next morning.

CHAPTER 15

I woke up, bought a cup of coffee, and went back up to my flat. The evening breeze had fumigated the inside. I called for maintenance to see about fixing the window, and informed them that I would cover the charge. Then for the next hour I puttied and repainted the wall, covering up all traces of defacement.

When I finished, I did not bother to shower, but rummaged through my closet for a pair of overalls, workman's boots, and a straw hat.

I dressed myself in the attire and drove out to a service station just outside of the Quarter. Roy, my mechanic, was up early, bending over a gutted V-8 engine when I pulled onto the lot.

Roy was a short colored man, with bowed legs and an elongated stomach. His oval shaped head was fattish, and balanced on a meaty axis of a neck.

I descended upon him and he stood up from the engine and greeted me with a firm handshake.

"Morning, Mr. Fletcher. Does your machine need some fixin'?"

"Probably, but we'll take care of that later. I came to take that Model A truck off your hands for a bit. I'll gladly pay for its use."

Roy swooshed a hand. "Aw, don't worry about it, Mr. Fletcher. She's running good, and got a full tank. Take her as long as you like."

"Thanks, Roy. All right if I borrow that pickax of yours?"

"Sure thing, boss. It's in the shop. You doin' some farmwork on the side or somethin'?"

"Something like that," I said.

I retrieved the ax, tossed it into the back of the truck, and set off toward River Road, a seventy-mile corridor that snaked along the Mississippi. I took the road past antebellum plantations and through the surviving farms. These were not the most prosperous years for the agricultural industry, and it was surprising they managed to get anything to grow out of the ground.

The air smelled of manure and smoke as I passed fields where laborers were hard at work burning post-harvest sugarcane. I

stopped and spoke with some of the laborers along the way.

A lot of them had noticed fancy cars had
been trafficking down the main road, who
they had figured were nothing but motor
gypsies. The farther up into Valerie, the
more details I got, until one worker informed me that he saw one of the cars coming out of the De Ponts' plantation up the
road.

The house was done in Greek Revival
style — fifty feet tall, with porches on all
sides. The locals told me that the De Pont
family was scarcely able to make it in the
sugar business when large sugar factories
had run most small mills out. Despite that,
they had been able to get by until recently,
when the spread of mosaic disease in the
crops had been too much and the family
abandoned the house a few years back.

I tugged the hayburner past the entrance
and up the street, where I parked it to the
side of the road. With the straw hat firmly
pulled over my head, I stepped out, and
retrieved the pickax from out of the back.

The next few hours I picked at the dirt in
the roadside ditch for no apparent reason,
while I whistled old blues songs I tried to
remember. When dusk came, I saw movement on the property for the first time.

Two figures were walking to a shed adjacent to the house. One of them stood in front of the shed and pushed back the sliding door. The darkness made it hard to see what was inside, until the front lights of a coupe lit up. I saw a machine pull out of the shed, where it stopped and waited for the other man to slide the door back into place and lock it. Once the man got into the passenger side, the car kicked up dust as it roared out of the lot and onto the main road. It didn't even stop to notice me as it sped off.

I waited a bit longer once the car had left before I tossed the ax in the cab and steered the truck back onto the road.

At the nearest call box, I phoned Brawley. Still doing late paperwork at the station, he said, "You know the police motto, 'If it ain't written down, it didn't happen.' "

"Well, if you want some more stuff to write up, meet me at my place as soon as you can break free. I might have found where Mallon is."

The rest of the drive into town after I had hung up, I thought over a possible fight plan. I sorted all of Mallon's faults and temperament. His greatest weakness was his one-track mind-set fueled by emotion rather than any sort of rational thinking. This was an amateur trait, and made him easy to be systematically picked apart. All it would require would be to dangle Mallon's current object of obsession in front of him, leaving him wide open.

I found Roy still messing with the engine when I dropped the truck off at the garage and took my lift to the apartment.

Brawley sat propped in a reclining chair in the courtyard when I arrived. He followed me up to the room, took a cigarette that I offered him out of a lacquered pine box, and glanced over an area map I folded out in front of him.

"That's where he's nested at, huh? No doubt that place is stock full of his plug-uglies armed for bear."

"I would think so. But Mallon is a fish out of water here. He thinks he's still in the big city. If we could divert his muscle into town, he'd be vulnerable."

"What are you thinking here?" Brawley questioned.

"A basic diversion. He ain't thinking straight with his hard-on for the girl. He'd send all the gorillas he has to go get her if he had the opportunity."

"You want to use the broad as bait?"

"I don't think we have to," I said. "You

think you can get a go-ahead from the station?"

"I don't know. Getting something with a judge's handwriting on it might be hard. The chief definitely will go for it. He's been puffin' ever since Mallon's hoods bumped off Flori. It ain't even about jurisdiction. I know the sheriff that works the St. James Parish, and he knows he didn't stay elected because of his looks."

"You get it squared away on your end, and tomorrow I'll see what kind of trouble I can stir up," I said.

After Brawley left, I spent the remainder of the evening cleaning the Colt. It had collected a significant amount of dirt in the barrel after I had dropped it upon being shot. Prior to me meeting Brawley, my knowledge of guns was at best sketchy. Brawley would take me on his days off out into the country and had me shoot at an assortment of targets until my marksmanship got to be mildly competent. He also showed me how to field strip the Colt for cleaning.

"Goddamn, you best start learnin' how to take care of your gun," he told me. "In this humidity you need to be cleanin' it all the time or you're going to find that when you need it, the only thing you'll be lucky enough to get coming out of its barrel is a pile full of rust."

I removed the slide lock, spring, barrel bushing, and barrel, and cleaned the powder and dirt out using a combination of a wire brush, toothbrush, and cotton swabs. I gave the parts a good but not excessive oiling, re-assembled it and wiped it down with a coarse cloth.

Satisfied with my work, I put the gun away, and lit a cigarette out on the gallery. My barometer showed the air pressure dropping, but the night remained clear, with only a mild wind that came from the northeast.

If things went well, by the end of tomorrow Zella would not need any more protection. That was my only interest in the matter. It was not my job to catch or punish bad guys. That was for the boys in blue. Yet there would be some personal satisfaction that went with seeing Mallon taken care of. His childish threats, insults, and ear-banging were nothing but annoyances. But having a cigar burned into my hand, and "ALL NIGGERS DIE" being carved into the wall of my home were more than that. And I'd be damned if Mallon got the best of me.

CHAPTER 16

The next morning, after I went out for breakfast, I found one of Mallon's plants standing on St. Ann's, dressed as a panhandler. He stood at six foot two, one hundred and ninety pounds, and was costumed in stained khakis and a shabby overcoat.

I moved toward him and said, "Since when did bums start wearing eighteen-karat gold watches and fancy shoes?"

Through gritted teeth he hissed, "I've had my fill of you!"

The man tore into his coat and pulled out a heavy revolver. I was close enough to grab his wrist with an unyielding lock and used the rest of my leverage to send my right fist down onto his collarbone like a fortified ax.

The bone snapped and the man shrieked as his right side went limp, causing the revolver to hit the concrete with a metallic clatter.

The turbulent movement sent crippling

pain lashing out from my wound. I clutched my side as I backed away from him. Endeavoring to keep the pain out of my voice, I said, "Go call your boss. I'm done risking my life over a woman, and I'm willing to get rid of her. He can pick the time and place, and he knows how to reach me. I'll be up in my flat waiting."

It required a calculated effort to get up to my room without giving in to the pain that boiled out of my side. With each step the agony cultivated new forms of distress, until I made it inside, downed half a bottle of aspirin, and plummeted onto the couch.

Mallon called twenty minutes later. "Your black ass and that dame better be out at the wharf at ten tonight." He paused before he ended with, "I want that book, too," and hung up.

At eight o'clock, I sat in the passenger seat of Brawley's '37 Chrysler Royal. In the back sat Ducan, a rookie in the vice unit, and McKenzie, a deputy sheriff for the St. James Parish. Brawley had not been amused with the sheriff only giving him one deputy. "I ain't kickin'," Brawley had said, "he's got loads of deputies that don't do nothin' but help old ladies across the street, and all he can free up is one?"

240

We parked off a side road to the main route that led to the plantation. Brawley had torn through the Royal's 700R4 tranny and made good time getting to our destination. Night came upon us as we arrived, and he picked the darkest spot to obscure the black-tinted machine.

We sat in silence at first. Restless, Brawley twisted the knobs on his Roamio radio, getting nothing but static and hair tonic commercials.

"Can't I listen to the radio without these stupid advertisements," he grumbled.

He switched the device off and leaned back into his seat. More silence. McKenzie used a pocket flash to read a science fiction magazine that had a half-naked Amazonian octopus woman with six arms and a robotic man necking with each other on the cover.

"Some reporter came into the station today," Brawley said. "Wanted to do some tragic piece on Ranalli."

"No kidding," I said.

"Says it was his editor's idea. Seems to think the public likes them kinda stories. So I gave him a few tales the readers would enjoy. Like how he used to beat up all them whores that were workin' for him. Told him about Brigette Leslie, who's a permanent resident up at the state asylum after she jumped on the crazy train from the seven-day grind he was working her."

"What'd he think of that?"

"He didn't like it so much," Brawley said. "He's like 'I can't sell that! Give me some dope I can work with here, buddy! Don't you got any shoot-out stories about him or a heat-packing moll?' I said he should stick to writing about the jazz. That's the new diversion from all the city's problems."

Nine o'clock rolled around and soon a convoy of headlights charged down the street ahead of us in a bellow of wound-up engines. A caravan of killers.

"And the ponies are off," Brawley said.

We let forty minutes pass before Brawley opened the door. "Me and the boys are going to sneak through the back. This being police business, Fletcher, I just want you to plant yourself out front. If anyone but us tries to go out the front or any of the side doors, you do what you got to do."

We crept down the side street and through the exterior property to the side of the plantation. Static filled the air, and made the hairs on my arms go erect. Far away, livid clouds sparked cyclically, but not bright enough or close enough to give away our position.

We split up as we came upon the house. I

broke off left toward the front, while they went up through the back entrance. No lights were coming from the plantation, nor could we see any lookouts or men canvassing the area.

In black togs, I blended into shadows and secured a spot behind a substantial oak tree near the front.

The oak not only provided me cover but gave me a clear vista of the front of the manor. I glimpsed inside the Favrile stained glass windows, with painted sugar stalks and palmetto leaves, and saw nothing. The house was destitute. The urge for a cigarette came to me, but smoking would draw too much attention, so I pushed the compulsion out of my head.

Zella's kiss had skipped in and out of my cranium since it had happened, and it chose this particularly inappropriate time to make itself known once more. I shook my head to clear it out and got interrupted by a hammering sound within the house. The windows flickered with the light of guns going off. The firing was unremitting, with only brief pauses for reloads. I held my own gun in the ready position and waited. The shelling from the interior kept its pace until an eruption from inside shook the building from the groundwork up.

Silence followed the explosion. The gun-fire stopped. I kept in idleness until I spot-ted movement behind the house. Not even needing to see the figure to know it had to be Mallon just by his awkward movements, I moved away from the oak and up to the front of the house and around the corner. Mallon was fleeing through the cane fields that lay ahead. I fired a shot in his direc-tion, but he ignored it and kept going. I started in after him.

I was intimate enough with my surround-ings to maneuver through the darkness. Mallon, however, seemed to be not so well off. He stumbled and zigzagged aimlessly. I narrowed the distance between us and sent him darting in the direction of the sugar mill. I fired at him once more as he entered the refinery. The shot missed him by inches.

I slowed up. I did not want to go in after him. If he wasn't armed, the mill would have many readily available things on hand that could be used as armaments.

I sized up the situation. His attack would be to find a place to stow himself while I went in looking for him like a dummy. He'd just need to wait for the right moment, and take me by surprise with whatever imple-ment of death he was able to get his hands on.

I approached the front of the mill, which was made of riveted steel girders and corrugated metal covered over by wood framing and brick. To the side of the building was a hefty wooden door made for machinery to pass through.

I waited nearby as the sound of an engine starting came from inside. I stepped to the side in time to see the wooden entrance door crumble and the menacing front end of a Ford AA dump truck tear itself out like a caged animal.

Mallon had busted out one of the front mounted headlights going through the door, and he was having trouble maneuvering without it. He caught sight of me and jerked the front end of the apparatus in my direction and accelerated toward me. I blasted three shots from the Colt and jumped aside into the dirt. I landed on my shoulder wrong and it screamed out in painful protest.

Two of the bullets I fired hit their mark. Mallon fell back from the wheel but kept his foot on the throttle. The truck bent to the left and with a mind of its own veered in the direction of an emptied irrigation ditch as if it saw the ditch as the most suitable place for it to fall in and die.

The machine swept in on the ditch at a

high speed and went off the edging embankment like it was going to take flight. Its weight and gravity made sure it adhered to the laws of physics by plucking the truck's front end down into a nosedive. The truck hit bottom and collapsed to its side with the harsh clanging rattle of smashed metal.

I staggered to the wreckage and saw Mallon dragging his ruined body along the bottom of the ravine, now littered with rotted burlap sacks of raw sugar that had spilled from the traumatized machine. Near the edge of the ditch, he flipped himself over onto his back. His blood-soaked hands were pressed tightly against his torn stomach.

Mallon didn't move when I approached him. The left side of his ruined face split open, and a cascade of blood seeped down it.

"You were right," he said with labor. "This ain't my climate. I'm used to making getaways in fast cars, not a goddamn dump truck."

"You did all right for yourself," I said.

He coughed, and blood brewed up out of his mouth. "I should have took your advice and stuck to the numbers. Haven't been thinking straight since I found out Storm was here. That night has haunted me for years and it all came rushing back. I figure

246

you know what happened after getting your hands on my book."

"I got my ideas, but I'd rather hear it from you," I said.

"I bet you would." He laughed, and more blood came out. "Not much time left for me. I guess I'm finished."

I waited for him to gather what little strength he had left. "For as long as I could remember, I never was 'normal,' as my folks would put it. When I got abducted by Storm, it was just him and me for nearly a week before you showed up. He treated me nice. Well, as nice as someone of his caliber could be. And I felt feelings I never felt before. That's why when you set me free that day, I didn't want to go. I knew he'd kill me, but I couldn't leave. After that I tried to stay the best I could for my folks' sake. I got the idea maybe if I wrote the supposed sinful things down, it'd get it out of my system. Then that bitch scrubwoman found the book, and after I stole it back, I knew I had to hide it. So I buried it. I always meant to go get it, but after my parents were killed, I got sidetracked."

"Why did you kill your parents?" I asked.

"Didn't have much of a choice. I would imagine they always knew something was wrong with me. But when my dad caught

247

me with another boy one day, things changed. I'd get beaten routinely, and it went up from there. Whatever love I had for them was gone. They were going to disown me and send me to a nuthouse. So one night while they were arguing over me in their room, I came in and shot them both. I covered it up best I could, and bribed the detective on the case. I offered him a big cut of the inheritance. After that, I took over the family business and started in on the numbers racket.

"But I couldn't forget Storm. I sent some of the best people to try to locate him. When they found him hiding in Boston, I left without thinking. You should've seen his face when I knocked on the door of the joint he was hiding out at. He didn't recognize me at first, until I told him who I was. He invited me in and acted like we were old friends. Said he never was going to harm me. I guess I got caught up in the moment, and I told him how I felt about him."

Mallon went into a fit of coughing, and by the amount of blood coming out, I knew he had minutes left in him.

"I don't know what happened after that," he continued. "My memory gets a bit fuzzy from all the blows Storm gave me. I remember laughing every time he hit me, because in some way I liked it. That seemed to really tick Storm off more, and he hit me so hard I blacked out. I woke up tethered to a chair, and saw Storm lighting a kerosene blow-torch. I recall him muttering that he was going to burn that queer pretty-boy face of mine right off. I don't remember much after that, except waking up in the hospital."

Mallon laughed. "Maybe my parents were right, I do belong in a nuthouse. Because no matter what he did to me, I still had feelings for him."

"Why were you so hell-bent on killing his daughter?" I asked. "Storm was dead, why couldn't you just leave it at that?"

"Someone else robbed me of the chance to make him pay! Somebody had to suffer for what was done to me, so it might as well be her. Like father, like daughter."

"She ain't nothing like her old man."

"Sure, she ain't! The apple never falls that far from the tree. She'll end up just —" He broke off, and looked out past me into nothing particular. Death came to him soon after, and his lifeless, mutilated head slumped to the side.

The inside of the plantation house was littered with corpses. I found Tommy O'Cahan lying just inside the back door with a chunk of his head missing, a frozen grimace on his face. There were more bodies in the main room near the stairs. The putrid smell of burnt flesh and bodies was nauseating.

The last quarter of the staircase had been blown to pieces. Midway up the stairs was McKenzie, covered in a fresh coat of bullets. Farther up was a singed torso of what I guessed was a man. The body would have been unrecognizable, but I recognized the immaculate shoes I witnessed Buzz Martin wearing a few nights earlier.

The first door in the hallway at the top of the stairs was propelled off its hinges. I went inside, and saw Brawley inside a cast-iron tub, holding his gun while clutching his right shoulder.

"What happened to you?" I asked.

"Big explosion, had to take cover," he said.

I helped him out of the tub, and on unsteady feet he stumbled out of the room and into the hall.

"What went on?" I asked.

"Hell went on. They were waiting for us when we came in. Made too much damn noise picking the lock. Opened the door and an entire goon squad was standing just on the other side. I knew they weren't going to let us leave alive, and I wasn't going to go out like a chump. I shot the closest one to me straight in the head and we bolted upstairs. McKenzie didn't make it. Bastards cut him in half before he could even get up the stairs. I took a hit myself in the arm, but Ducan and me were able to secure ourselves in the bathroom. The elevated position helped our odds, and I got to picking most of them off. I sent Ducan to check the back rooms to see if Mallon was hiding out there. That's when one of them got the cute idea of running up the stairs with a live pineapple to throw at me. He almost made it before I saw him. He had the pin in his mouth and was about to toss it by the time I shot half his arm off. I didn't wait to see what happened, and dove straight for the tub. I guess I hit the bottom too hard, because I blacked out for a few. Came to just a few moments before you got here."

"Glad you didn't shoot me when I came in," I said.

"Damn near did, but the rod is on empty. Best I could do was throw it at you."

"Why didn't you?"

"I figured it was you. If there was still any more of them alive, they wouldn't have come through the door like that. They would toss another one of them bombs in the room and called it good. By the way, you're the worst backup I've ever had. What the hell took you so damn long?"

"I was busy going after Mallon," I said.

"Where is he?"

"In a ditch behind the house," I said.

"I guess this evening didn't turn out so bad after all," Brawley said.

I helped Brawley get back down to the ground floor, where he called it in. A few minutes later Ducan came in through the front door.

"Where you been?" Brawley yelled.

"I was chasing after someone. I went and checked the rooms like you told me to. Didn't find Mallon, but in the last room I saw someone climbing down off the balcony. I don't know who he was. When he got to the ground, and saw me on the gallery, he fired a few shots. I returned fire, and hit him, but he still ran off. When I got down so I could go after him, I followed the blood trail the best I could in this light, but it got too dark to track. I didn't have a flash on me, but I can tell you, he ain't going to go far. I think I got him in a bad area. The blood was real dark."

"You did good," Brawley said. "You got a cigarette, Fletcher?"

I shook loose a cigarette for him, and we waited till the sound of far-off sirens came.

252

CHAPTER 17

It took days for the officials to clear the plantation. Upon canvassing the area, deputies found on the main road the remains of a local, Leland Wendell. He'd been run over repeatedly by his own Chevrolet Series DB Master Commercial truck. The authorities believed it was a sure shot that the carnage was the aftermath of a reckless escape by the man Ducan had shot. Wendell's wife, Bernadine, had been found five miles down the road. It was reckoned that she'd been tossed out of the truck going over fifty.

The truck was unearthed off of River Road just inside New Orleans city limits. It had been rammed into an oak tree. Nobody was found in the wreckage, but a large amount of blood was found in the truck's interior. There was an additional blood trail that left the truck and went to a roadside police call box a quarter mile up the street. A phone history of all the numbers called from the call box was made, but turned up little. The only number they got for that day was unlisted, and upon calling it, they found it to be disconnected.

Word got to us as soon as the sheriff and deputies arrived that the rest of Mallon's men had driven themselves right into a police chopper squad. Their machines were torn into till there was nothing left but the chassis and wheels. Mallon should have prepared his gorillas for such an ambush, but he wasn't thinking straight. His carelessness was why he ended up dead.

The deputies on-site did their best to barricade the ensuing news, but to no avail. The story hit the front page of the paper and was burned on there for days. The media found a new hero in Brawley, and played him up as the new crusader of crime.

I made an appearance at the Department of Justice, where I surrendered written documentation that I had discharged my weapon and the result was the death of Mallon. Mallon being deemed a dangerous criminal and the circumstances leading to him being fired upon made it obvious self-defense. Yet I was told they were going to review the matter very seriously to see if it was in fact reasonable use of deadly force. I knew little would come of it. My involvement in the raid was being underwritten and concealed from the media, for political reasons, no less. The way the department saw it, a colored man taking out Mallon as opposed to one of their own was upsetting to them. But being kept out of the papers was fine by me. The few times I ever did make it in them, the kindest way they referred to me was as "the Negro."

A day after I made my report to the Department of Justice, District Attorney Emerson came a-calling.

It was a repeat of the last time I got called into Emerson's office. I sat back in silence while Jim Prescott did all the talking. The difference was that this time it wasn't just Emerson in the room. Chief of Police Golik and Mayor Maestri were there as well.

Mayor Maestri prided himself on being a moral politician, yet his frequent visits to the city's brothels were a secret to few. When he publicly got caught coming out of such a questionable establishment, he stated he went there for "investigation" purposes into the city's sex trade.

Emerson, Golik, and Maestri took turns throwing out accusations and threats, which Prescott refuted. Golik accused me of overstepping my bounds by being involved in the takedown of Mallon. Prescott's rebuttal was that I was working directly under the supervision of Brawley, and that any complaints he had, he'd have to take up with his own officer.

This led to the tactic they always went for, the threat of suspending my license. Prescott refuted the threat, stating it was not their decision but the State Licensing Board's. He reminded them that they were currently on not so good terms with the board. The board had grown weary of the police frequently overreaching their authority by suspending licenses without their approval, and their perpetual bullying tactics to do so. He went on to say that the board would dismiss any case they brought against me, since they had no direct evidence that I had violated the terms of any agreement.

When the meeting reached its closing, all allegations from them had been roadblocked. Emerson said little. He sat mostly in silence and I watched as the color drained out of his face. He did not have a favorable reputation as a competent DA as it was, and allowing me to come out of this unscathed, he almost certainly knew that by the next election he would be railroaded out of his position like so many DAs before him.

He spoke up only after receiving ghastly looks from Maestri. "Let's be reasonable here, Prescott," he said. "I'm sure Mr. Fletcher means well, but it would just be best if he ceased what he is currently doing."

"It would be the best for whom?" Prescott asked. "If you cannot see the benefits my client provides, that is your business. Now I'm not going to bore you gentlemen with the litany of squandered opportunities over something as trivial as skin color, but suffice to say, in my briefcase I have a signed letter from Detective Brawley stating what a valuable resource my client is. I'm sure if this made its way to the papers, people would be interested to know that, especially when it was written by a party who has received a proportionate amount of recent public acclaim."

Emerson said nothing. His poignant face tilted down at his desk, while Golik and Maestri looked on in disgust.

That evening Emerson did a nine-point Olympic dive out of his third-story apartment window onto Rampart Street.

Prescott notified me of the event early the next morning. He said that the city should think about renaming Rampart after him. He thought it would only be fitting, since the street was the only sort of impact Emerson had ever made in his life.

■ ■ ■ ■

I called JaRoux before he left his bait shop and told him to pass on to the women that I would be picking them up at the pier the following evening. When I arrived on Pratt Drive, the officers that had been planted there after Mallon's men gave the place the works were gone.

Zella's house had been professionally searched by Mallon's men in an endeavor to find anything that could tell them where she was.

I used the phone to call Lily Everhard and asked her if she could do her best fixing the place up by the next day. Everhard was a middle-aged mulatto woman who on occasions scoured my own apartment.

I made another call to a locksmith and asked him to come out and replace the entrance door lock that had been damaged in the break-in.

At seven the next evening I waited in my car and watched as the boat carrying Zella and Aunt Betty glided up to the pier. I got out and helped them stow their things in the car. They said little on the drive, outside of Zella stating how strange it felt being back in the city again.

I helped with their bags up to the place, and I could see they were both a bit worried at what they were going to find inside. I had informed them earlier that the house had been ransacked, and upon opening the door, they were greeted with the revelation that the house ended up being cleaner than when they had left. Everhard was very capable at what she did.

Aunt Betty retired soon after, while Zella offered to brew me coffee. I took her up on her offer, and set out to the bathroom to wash up. The sticky humidity of the swamps always left me in an unclean state.

I opened the wrong door. Instead of the lavatory, I got welcomed with the image of Aunt Betty standing with her back to the door in nothing but her underwear and a brassiere as she changed into her night attire. The horrific scene would be enough to make even the most fertile of men impotent.

In the course of sealing the door on the unpleasantness, I spotted something that did interest me.

I found Zella in the kitchen. She too had changed into her nightwear, a negligee. Pouring the coffee into two cups, she looked up and saw me.

"You all right?" she asked. "You look like you just crawled out of a grave."

"I'm fine," I said, taking a seat near the table.

"How's your injury?"

"It's fine. It hasn't got infected, but I ripped a few stitches out not too long ago."

She handed me a cup too hot to drink. I set it on the table while Zella straddled my knee.

"You have been a tremendous help to me," she said. "I am very grateful." She leaned into me and rested her hands on my shoulders. "So what can I do to repay you?"

Tired of her teasing, I pushed her off me, stood up, and kicked the chair I had been sitting on back.

"I don't like being toyed with," I said. "That might work with other suckers, but not me, understand? As for repaying me, I'll send you a bill."

I walked out, nearly taking her front door with me as I left. On the drive to my flat, I knew there was no chance I'd be able to sleep, as irked as I was. I took a detour to the Saint-Pierre Boxing Gym.

I was pleased to see that the exercise room was still open. It was not uncommon for them to stay open past working hours for a boxer that needed to do some extra training before an upcoming bout.

I stripped off my jacket and shirt so that I

was dressed only in my undershirt and trousers, and set to work on one of the heavy bags. My wound acted up, but I ignored it. I kept up hitting the bag with powerful punches until my arms went numb and I had to wrap around the suspended bag itself for support.

The spasms in my arm were intense enough that I could barely grip the steering wheel of my machine when I left, let alone the doorknob to my place. I stripped, showered, and went to sleep as soon as my head collided with the pillow.

CHAPTER 18

I pulled onto Pratt Drive the next morning. I knocked on the door and Aunt Betty opened it up about three inches.

"Zella is not here," she said. "She left early to see about getting another singing job."

"That's okay; it's you I want to talk to."

She opened the door the rest of the way. "You saw, didn't you?"

I jerked a nod and followed her into the house. She took a seat in the living room and asked, "You got a cigarette?"

Her old marm act vanished. She substituted it with a slight hint of a Queens accent. I shook loose a cigarette from my deck and she reached for it.

"I wanted to get rid of that tattoo. I didn't even want it. It was Bill that made me get it," she said, accepting my light.

"You are probably wondering what this is all about."

"I just want to know why you are passing

yourself off as your daughter's aunt, and why you went by your mother's name when you were with Storm."

She puffed out a plume of smoke from her lungs. "I left home when I was sixteen to go to New York and be a dancer. My mother did not approve, but that didn't matter to me. I was very good. Got me an agent that helped me get work. Trouble was he didn't like my name, Betty. I think it was because his ex-wife was named Betty. So I threw some names out and I guess the first one off the top of my head was Frieda, my mother's name and my middle name. He liked it and so Frieda Rae was my performing name. It was also the name I went by when I met Bill.

"Bill was everything a young gal that didn't know any better could ever want. Ruggedly handsome, unpredictable, wild, the works. I fell hard for that boy. It was only after we were going steady that the beatings started and I got pregnant. I thought for sure I wasn't going to have it but once Bill found out I was expecting, he just hit me everywhere else but the stomach.

"When Zella was born, I knew I had to leave, if not for my own sake, for Zella's. I went back to my ma's place. She was not content with the whole situation. My ma was a very religious woman, and having a child out of wedlock was a sin as far as she saw it. That's not including that I was a dope fiend at that point. I never took the stuff until the beatings. Bill busted me up so bad my back hurt so much, I couldn't even get out of bed without taking something for it. I tried to clean up for Zella, but I couldn't get off the hop. I knew I was no good for her, so about a year in I left her with my mother. She raised Zella as her own child, while I was drifting town to town looking for my next kick. It was not until I got word that my mother was sick that I cleaned up and came here to see her. She introduced me to Zella as her aunt Betty. It wasn't much of a stretch, because I could pass as her aunt. All the stuff I was taking took a toll on my beauty."

She extended one of her aged hands in front of her and looked at it with despondent eyes. "I was very beautiful once. I got it from my mother, who was beautiful as well."

"Yes, you were a real peach," I said.

She sighed. "When my mother died, I moved in with Zella, and that's how it's been."

"Until you saw Storm in town," I said.

She showed no emotion. "Yes. I was out

264

shopping one afternoon and saw him harassing the owner of a stand I frequented. He was asking the man about me. I thought he was going to kill the poor man, but instead he kicked over one of the man's stands. I didn't know what to do. I kept hidden, and then followed him in my car. He didn't see me because he kept his head low as he was walking down the street, knocking people over that were in his way. When he got to a cabstand, I followed him to the place he was staying. I found out what room he was at, and I was going to confront him, tell him to leave, but I got afraid and left."

"Shortly after that," I said, "Zella must've called or told you I had visited her and told her I was in contact with Storm and left it up to her if she wanted to have a meeting with him."

"I know Zella, she would've met him. I could not allow her to meet that monster," she said.

"So you went back to his place," I continued, "and left a note saying you were Zella and that you wanted to meet him in the park. While he was sitting on the bench waiting for your daughter, you came from behind and shot him."

"I don't regret what I did," she said. "I was not going to let that brute corrupt her.

It is enough that she inherited some of his wickedness, it did not need to be extended by his influence. He would dominate her the same way he did with all the women that made the mistake of coming across his path."

"I understand," I said.

"I suppose you are going to pass this on to the police."

"What would be the point? They wouldn't believe it coming from me. Even if they did, they'd put the kid gloves on you, being a frail woman and especially since Storm was a cop killer."

"You are not as bad as I thought you were, if that means anything," she said.

I shrugged. "It might. Do you still have the gun?"

"Yes," she said. She left the room for a moment and came back with a .38 Special snubby, and handed it to me.

"I didn't even know how to use one until Storm taught me. Said was for my own protection. He said I should stick to the snub-nosed revolver so it wouldn't get stuck in my clothes if I had to pull it out in an emergency. Funny, if he never taught me that kind of stuff, he'd probably still be alive."

I snapped the barrel open and saw that

one of the six cylinders had been spent.

"You better let me keep this," I said.

About to say something in protest, she changed her mind and simply nodded.

I stuffed the gun into my pocket and asked, "Why haven't you told Zella yet who you really are?"

"Who am I? Her mother? Just because I may have given birth to her does not make me her mother. It was my own mother that raised her when I could not. She has turned out to be for the most part a very lovely young lady and that was my mother's doing. I was just a bad egg. I do not have the right to call myself Zella's mother. I won't take that away from the real woman that mothered her. The only thing I can say I'm proud of is keeping her away from Bill."

I had gained a new respect for Aunt Betty. I left the house and tossed the gun she used to end Bill Storm's life of terror into the canal. She had her predicaments, but her maternal instincts for what was best for her child had to be respected.

I emptied the remainder of the afternoon attempting to unwind in my flat. I played an assortment of records and sat out on the gallery, smoking heavily. The phone had rung at numerous times, but I ignored it, until its metallic drumming grew tiresome. Irritated, I was about to pull the line out of the jack when I chose to just answer it instead.

"Someone wants to see you this evening," an unemotional voice said over the line.

"I'm not in the mood to meet with anyone this evening. Tomorrow would be better."

"He will be dead by tomorrow."

"Tonight will be fine then," I said.

I took the directions of where to meet the person down and at seven that evening I stood at the Toulouse Street wharf. An escort waited for me and I followed him up the gangplank onto a three-deck stern-wheeler. The escort made me wait above deck until the rotating paddle blades tore into the sepia-colored Mississippi and propelled the floating boat away from shore. I then was taken below deck, where my escort knocked on one of the cabin doors.

The door opened and an aged man with wire-brush whiskers and carrying a brown leather doctor's bag stepped out.

"I'm pleased you could make it," he said. "I am Dr. Langley. I spoke to you on the phone. You may speak to the patient for a short while. I have not given him any sedatives for some time so he may speak to you of sound mind. The patient has suffered a grave injury and now infection has set in, and it is my prognosis that he will not make it past this evening. When the pain gets to be too great, I will come in and the meeting will be adjourned so that I may sedate him. Do we have an understanding?"

I said we did. The doctor pulled a cigar wrapped in cellophane out of his pocket and followed my escort above deck while I went into the cabin.

The tainted smell that occurs when death is imminent inundated the room. The cabin was vacant except for a bed where only the head of a man, propped up on pillows, was exposed.

The man's flaxen hair was cropped short. His features were sharp, as if chiseled from stone. I had never seen the face before, but in some way I had. The comic section of the day's paper was resting below his chest.

"You look a little uneasy there," he said in a hoarse voice. "What's the matter with you? Never seen a dead man before?"

"You're not dead yet, Ranalli. Though I had been told otherwise," I said.

"I wouldn't be too disappointed. I'm finished. That cop was a damn good shot. Doc is a bit stumped on how I've managed to last this long."

"Maybe such things as death don't apply

to you," I said. "Like Rasputin. He too had a knack for not dying."

"I ain't like him," he said. "All them theatrics was Mallon's doin'. That kid should've been in show business or a circus. He'd fit right in with the bearded lady and the elephant man."

"Seems like you two made a good team, and I'm interested in knowing how it all transpired," I said.

Ranalli tried to force a grin. "I thought you would be. Why I had you come."

Through the course of an hour Ranalli told me his tale, in sporadic pieces, resting when the pain was too significant. I had to put the rest together myself when on the brink of the end, the doctor came in and doped Ranalli up.

It went something like this:

After the racketeering indictment and being pressured into going stoolie, Ranalli was left in bad shape. He could not even fence goods without the hammer and saws breathing down him. Mallon had been trying to persuade him to bring the numbers game to the city, but in his predicament, it was impossible. That's when they came up with the scheme.

Mallon was having his own troubles at the time. A rival syndicate run by Jack Stein was moving in on his territory. Mallon had a meeting with Stein, and convinced him that if they combined forces and took Ranalli on, New Orleans would be the prime area for running numbers. Since there was no competition at the time, it was up for the taking, and they would split the take.

Stein was more than eager to go along with Mallon's proposal, and sent his best men out to aid Mallon. When Mallon bombed the New Orleans Hotel, Ranalli and his mugs were not even in the building. They had been tipped off by Mallon, and the bodies the police recovered were men that had been already killed by Ranalli a few hours before.

Ranalli's counterattack on Mallon was staged. Mallon and his men left the building long before the truck full of explosives arrived. Mallon had left six of Stein's men to watch the place, and when the truck exploded, it was the end of them.

With minor police assistance, Ranalli got rid of the rest of Stein's men, who were hiding out in the city.

"It was like shooting fish in a barrel," Ranalli said. "Mallon gave us their exact locations and rooms."

It did not take long for Stein to get word

of what happened, and he demanded immediate reimbursement. At that point, his demands fell on deaf ears. With his most prominent regiment dead, Stein was a deer caught in the headlights. Ranalli stated that it was definitely Stein that killed Mallon's right-hand man, Devland, and that the move was reckless. Devland was well connected with several big Irish gangs. He was once a member of the White Hand gang before the Black Hand took over the Brooklyn waterfront.

Once Ranalli had made his staged attack, it was time to create his cover. "See, the only time I was ever printed was when I got busted doin' a hold-up job in Atlanta. I was only twenty, but see, the cop that processed me was a crooked bastard, and after shovin' enough jack his way he had the prints switched with the prints of a pal of mine. He wasn't planning on living long because he was a lunger, got it from the Spanish flu. But he was a tough bird, I'll give him that. He somehow managed to keep living. But he was damn near dead when I found him in the medical ward. He begged me to kill him, so what kind of pal would I be if I didn't do as he asked?"

Ranalli smuggled the body and strategically burned him before propping the body in the car.

"See, faking your death is the easy part. People do it all the time to avoid debts or having the wife keep tappin' them for alimony. But all them mugs don't plan ahead enough, and get themselves caught. See, you got to go all the way and cover your tracks real good. Gotta be creatin' a new look, identity, the whole works."

As soon as police confirmed that Ranalli was dead, he went under the knife, and his features were reshaped. He used chemicals to bleach over his naturally black hair.

The plan was that once Ranalli had recovered, Mallon would have already instituted the numbers game and Ranalli would silently run the show in the shadows while Mallon returned to New York.

In New York, Mallon wouldn't have to worry too much over NOPD pursuing him, because they were wise enough to know that doing so would greaten the chances of their unlawful involvement with Stein's men being revealed. Even if they tried to hang Flori's murder on him, Mallon could bust free of it. His lawyers could hang the murder on Ranalli, and expose it as an obvious frame-up job, which in a way, it was.

But none of the plans worked out that way. Mallon had put his commitments to the side and focused on his crusade to find Zella Storm.

"I would have killed the broad if I knew it'd cause Mallon to louse things up," Ranalli said.

"Why didn't you kill her if you were working with Mallon from the beginning?" I asked.

"It was too good of a cover not to. If the cops started scratchin' their asses and wonderin' what brought this about between Mallon and me, the girl would be the ideal root of it all. Men fought entire wars over a single broad. Besides, they never would have bought it being over the numbers racket, because the cops knew I was locked up tighter than Kelsey's nuts and I'd never be able to do the numbers even if I wanted to."

Upon his recovery, and seeing that nothing had been done, Ranalli went to Mallon at the plantation house to knock some sense into him, before Brawley and his men had busted in.

Ranalli was able to secure himself upstairs before the action started. He did not want his identity compromised, even after the work on his face. Brawley had seen Ranalli in person and he was no fool.

He kept himself hidden in one of the back

274

rooms until Officer Ducan arrived. Ranalli thought about killing Ducan as soon as he came into the room, but he knew that would draw Brawley's attention.

"If I had a shiv on me, I would've waited and slit that flatfoot's throat," Ranalli said. "Instead I go scaling down the gallery like a boob and got shot for it."

"How'd you make your escape from him?" I asked.

"I think it was all the dope I was on from the face work that kept me from droppin'. I got to the road in time to jack a car full of hillbillies that were coming by. It was some couple. Pops wasn't cooperative, so I pistol-whipped him and threw him out. He tried to get up and go after me when I got in his rig, so I plowed over him and popped it into reverse just to make sure he didn't get back up again. Wifey kept screaming, so I tossed her out a few miles down. I read in the paper she's a cripple now. That's too bad. Was hopin' for the best."

"I doubt it troubles you that much," I said.

"I ain't that heartless. That was a bad way to go for any dame. I wasn't in sound mind, being shot and all, and her yappin' and flailing around wasn't helping any. I reckon I should've slowed down before I tossed her out, but if the cops were chasin' after me,

275

that might've given them enough time to catch up. But I sent her some roses for her troubles. Them weeds weren't cheap, neither."

Ranalli must have seen the look on my face.

"Hey, where the hell do you get off lookin' at me like that! Don't you go foolin' yourself that you're any better than me, because you ain't. Like them cops that think that because they got a badge they got a legal right to kill people. Killing is killing in my book. Look at what they did to Pretty Boy Floyd. He was just running away, and them cops and FBI slaughtered him. I bet every one of them went home thinking they were the hero."

"You seem to think you got everyone figured out," I said.

"That's because people ain't that hard to figure out," he said. "Except guys like me. See, the popular talk is that we all come from a bad upbringing or something. That ain't it at all. My folks were pretty decent. They were Roman Catholics, made all us kids attend mass regularly. They didn't beat us or nothing, hell, they didn't even really yell at us."

"What went wrong, then?" I asked.

"Nothin' went wrong. They ain't nothin'

276

wrong with wantin' to make a buck, it's better than starvin'. My old man was poor when he came to this country, worked himself to death and died poor. You'd have to be pretty dumb to think I was goin' to do the same. So some people get killed along the way, ain't like most of them didn't have it comin' a hundred times over."

"What about all them innocent folks you killed?" I asked.

"Nobody's innocent. And let's say some people are, that's just how it goes. Like all them innocent German folks that got killed in the Great War. See, nobody ever talks about those people. Hell, how about all them non-whites that get strung up and lynched by the cops and all them innocent folks you're getting mushy about? For all you know, that hick I ran over with the truck went out every Saturday with his bedsheet-wearing pals and killed a few niggers for kicks."

"Yeah, and he could've been a preacher at the local church that helped the kids with their homework," I said.

"So what, that ain't the point. People these days like bad-mouthing those of us that were bootlegging the booze, but who was the one buying the stuff? Things ain't no different now, it's the same innocent folks that are paying for the whores and throwing their dough away playin' the cards. As for the drugs, that's Uncle Sam's fault when he made heroin illegal and left all them folks that'd been legally using the junk for years out in the lurch."

Ranalli did his best to mask the pain, but it overcame him. The doctor stepped in, gave him a morphine shot and concluded the interview, indefinitely.

I stood on the Toulouse Street wharf and watched as the paddle steamer drew away from the wharf and headed down the river toward the gulf.

In the same coffee shop Storm had come to me in, I spent the morning downing cups of coffee and writing up what Ranalli had told me on carbon paper for duplicate copies. When I had finished the report, I paid, and set out to my flat. At the corner of St. Ann and Royal, I came upon Brawley's Chrysler Royal with one of the front tires parked up on the curb.

In the driver's seat sat a healthy-sized woman, with golden hair and ivory white skin. Tamara Brawley.

I waved to her as I bent down to the passenger seat, where Brawley sat with his arm securely strapped into a sling.

"Was just about to take off," Brawley said. "The missus has been pestering me to take her to the show. I want to see my boy James Cagney, but she wants to see some romantic Clark Gable nonsense. Thought you might come along. Two against one and our chances of seeing ol' Jimmy are high."

"You should let her see what she wants," I said. "She deserves it, putting up with you."

"Traitor. I thought we were square. And after all I've done for you. Giving that mouthpiece of yours a solid recommendation."

"That helped a lot. Did Golik reprimand you for it?"

"Oh, the hell with Golik. He called me into his office, read me the riot act, but not like it did him any good. I was loopy from the drugs the doc gave me, so I just said, 'yes-sir' here and there, and left."

"All the same, I appreciate what you did. Why I bothered writing you up some reading material, but I wouldn't do anything with it — nobody will believe you."

I handed him a copy of the report. At first he was going to toss it aside, but after a cursory glimpse he began leafing through it. He was still reading it when Tamara, impatient, floored the car off the curb and away from me. She drove down the street, cutting off a car full of churchgoers that were en route to the St. Louis Cathedral. One of them stuck their head out the window and spouted off language that I doubted St. Peter would have approved of.

I had written up a bill and sent it over to Zella's residence. My response to it came a day later with a phone call from Zella asking me to meet her at a new club she was singing at on Bourbon.

The club was no different than the previous ones, with a crowd spilling all the way out into the entrance. I plowed my way to the bar as she got onstage.

She was wearing her standard slinky black dress, but her performance was not her normal stock. She didn't stay in a fixed position like she usually did, but moved around, and even flirted a bit with the crowd, giving them sultry looks. It was not the greatest performance I'd ever seen, but by far her best.

She again met me at the bar when she had finished. "I'd say you actually looked alive up there," I said.

She laughed. "Lot's changed, I suppose. A lot of weight has come off me. Some finality with my dad, and thanks to you, I don't have to worry about people trying to kill

280

me. Plus, I'm getting more comfortable with myself onstage, you know?"

"Yeah, I know," I said.

"Let me say good-bye to some people, and you can take me home."

Fifteen minutes later we stepped into my car. She pulled an envelope out of her purse and handed it over to me. "This should be enough."

I opened it up, and saw a stack of bills. I counted it out. "This is way more than what I charged you for. What'd you do, put your house up for sale to get this bundle?"

"Hey, don't you be askin' where I got it, because I ain't going to tell. We'll just say I recently received an inheritance."

I gave her a stern look.

"Just take the damn money, will you. You more than earned it."

Reluctantly, I grabbed a leather brief bag from out of the back, and pulled out a receipt form. I filled it out, and had her sign off, telling her it was just protection against the IRS.

When we were on our way, she said, "I heard you visited my mom, I mean, my aunt Betty."

"So you do know," I said.

"Of course I do. Can't keep something like that a secret, especially from your own daughter. I figured it out the minute my mom, or I guess my grandma, introduced her as my aunt, since she never talked about having a sister. I also know she killed my dad. I knew it the minute I found out he was killed. The cincher was the note saying it was me wanting to meet him."

"Very perceptive of you," I said.

"Funny, I was kind of expecting you to be more surprised when I told you this."

"That's because I ain't. Done this job long enough to know things are often not as they first appear, and they just spell themselves out with time and I guess a little prodding. Sure, you might get some twisted schemes, but the motives behind them are basic enough, and easy to spot."

"So you knew this all along?"

"Not the particulars — I had to let things play out to get them, and now I have. Your mother's 'Aunt Betty' act wasn't foolin' anyone, because she overdid it, and so did you."

"I don't get you," she said.

"Sure, you do. I know when a woman is legitimately interested in me, and you aren't, or at least not in that way. So when you happened to tell me good night while standing in your underwear, it was a tip-off. Then it was followed by that kiss you gave me. It stuck in my head, because it was so random, since you showed no buildup to it. The sealer was when you were about to give me a jump in the kitchen."

"But why would I do all that if I wasn't interested?"

"I don't think I have to begin to tell you the control women have when sex comes into play. You don't even have to really give it out, just tease a guy enough, and they can turn into clay for you to mold. I'm not going to say your motives behind it were sinister, because you were just trying to look out for your mother. You wanted me just for protection, but in case I caught on, you also wanted to make sure you had some control."

"You're pretty shrewd," she said as we pulled to the front of her house. "But you're wrong about something."

"What's that?"

"I was sort of interested in you. See, you fascinate me. When I first saw you, I thought you were just a big, dumb lug, but you ain't. But it's your violence that turns me off. It doesn't just come out in your sleep. I wouldn't say you are tortured over it, because by all accounts you seem content with your destructive tendencies. That's where we differ, you see. I know I got a temper, but I try to better myself. I guess what I'm saying is, I could never really feel safe around a guy like you."

I didn't say anything. There was nothing to say to something like that. I watched her as she stepped out of the car, walked up to her door, and went in without looking back.

The next few days I caught up on paperwork and filing. I was happy to close things out, since I was not pleased with myself at the work I had done. I'd grown too confident and comfortable in my profession so that it led to the slippery path of being careless. It was only because of Emerson's legal posturing, Brawley's support, and luck that I was not going up on charges.

I had indirectly caused the death of Devland and his men by handing their whereabouts over to Stein. At the time, I was not aware that Stein was capable of such actions, but I knew he was dangerous.

Then there were the two men I had gunned down, one of whom I hadn't even reported. An honest man I'm sure would have come clean over the poacher's death, knowing it was justified self-defense. But a simple case of self-defense could be manipulated into a murder charge, especially if the victim was white and the perpetrator happened to be colored. Jails were full of coloreds sent up on lesser things. It wasn't hard to seeing myself sitting in front of an all-white jury, being made an example of.

I got away with Mallon's death because Mallon was publicly shown to be a threat, and because of the department doing all they could to keep my involvement under wraps.

Then there was the illegal entry, mingling with criminals, withholding information from authorities, and other laws I broke or chose to ignore with reckless abandon. As justified as these actions might have been, in front of a judge I would lose all credibility.

I had barely skimmed by this time and only a fool would keep going in the direction I was. A lot of rope was given to me, enough to hang myself on, and that's precisely what I was sure they would be waiting for.

The only solution was to lay low. I had enough money saved up, combined with what Zella gave me. I wouldn't have to take a case for a few months, not that I currently had any cases to take. When the money started to get low, I would have to make the decision on whether or not to continue the trade.

With that settled, I cooked dinner. A

knock came on the door when I had finished eating. I answered it and saw Ida standing outside in a red lace evening dress, a suitcase positioned next to her.

"Where have you been?" I asked.

"Mallon hid me all the way out at Baton Rouge in some second-rate dive. When I read what happened to him, I laid low, and caught a bus out here. I'll be taking another bus tomorrow back to New York. I'm in no real hurry to get there, though."

"Well, you have a safe trip and all," I said.

Her lips went into a pout. "You can at the very least be a gentleman and invite me in for a drink before I shove off."

"I ain't a gentleman," I said.

"That's for sure. Come on, how about it?"

I stepped out of the way and ushered her in with my hand. I set about rummaging the cabinets for a bottle of bourbon I kept around for guests. I poured her out a glass. She had made herself comfortable in one of the chairs when I handed it over to her.

"It's strange," she said, taking a unlady-like portion of the contents in her glass. "A brute like you not even attempting to make a move on me. Does me being a former whore disgust you?"

"Why would it?"

"I don't know. A lot of people are. Not

286

that I'm ashamed of it, it was good money, and trust me, I earned it."

"So you've told me," I said. "Anyway, this has been a real delight, but I'm going to bed. You can finish your drink and help yourself out. Don't think about casing the joint, I don't got nothin' worth hocking."

I had nearly stepped into my bedroom when she said, "You want me to join you?"

I twisted back to her. "Join me where?"

She stood up from the chair and said, "In your bed, dummy!"

I didn't say anything. She must've seen the confusion on my face.

"Look here. I don't like you much, but it's been a long time comin' since I had some attention. I'm sure it's been a while for you, too. So I'm offerin' us both a chance to get some release, see."

In the course of her talking, her hands by some means had made their way to my belt, which she slipped off with the ease of someone who had a lot of practice taking the belts off men.

I stood outside the door like a chump as she went into the bedroom, slipped out of her dress and propped herself on top of the bed in a position that could only be described as pornographic.

"Make sure to shut the light off when you

come in. I don't want to look at that face of yours," she said.

ABOUT THE AUTHOR

Grant Bywaters has worked as a licensed private investigator. He now works security at the Portland Airport and is currently finishing his Bachelor's degree in psychology at Portland State University. Bywaters lives outside of Portland, Oregon. *The Red Storm* is his first novel.

The employees of Thorndike Press hope you have enjoyed this Large Print book. All our Thorndike, Wheeler, and Kennebec Large Print titles are designed for easy reading, and all our books are made to last. Other Thorndike Press Large Print books are available at your library, through selected bookstores, or directly from us.

For information about titles, please call:
  (800) 223-1244

or visit our Web site at:
  http://gale.cengage.com/thorndike

To share your comments, please write:
  Publisher
  Thorndike Press
  10 Water St., Suite 310
  Waterville, ME 04901